Whose dark or troubled mind will you step into next? Detective or assassin, victim or accomplice? How can you tell reality from delusion when you're spinning in the whirl of a thriller, or trapped in the grip of an unsolvable mystery? When you can't trust your senses, or anyone you meet; that's when you know you're in the hands of the undisputed masters of crime fiction.

Writers of the greatest thrillers and mysteries on earth, who inspired those that followed. Their books are found on shelves all across their home countries – from Asia to Europe, and everywhere in between. Timeless tales that have been devoured, adored and handed down through the decades. Iconic books that have inspired films, and demand to be read and read again. And now we've introduced Pushkin Vertigo Originals – the greatest contemporary crime writing from across the globe, by some of today's best authors.

So step inside a dizzying world of criminal masterminds with **Pushkin Vertigo**. The only trouble you might have is leaving them behind.

CRUSH

FRÉDÉRIC DARD

PUSHKIN VERTIGO

Pushkin Vertigo
71–75 Shelton Street
London, WC2H 9JQ

Original text © 1959 Fleuve Editions,
département d'Univers Poche, Paris

First published in French as *Les Scélérats* in 1959

Translation © Daniel Seton, 2016
First published by Pushkin Vertigo in 2016

1 3 5 7 9 8 6 4 2

ISBN 978 1 782271 98 7

Text designed and typeset by Tetragon, London
Printed and bound by CPI Group (UK) Ltd, Croydon CRO 4YY

www.pushkinpress.com

For Claire
and Philippe-Gérard
This "musty old smell"…
Affectionately,
F.D.

ONE

Léopoldville: a funny sort of name for a funny-looking sort of place. It's our town, and apparently it was built by a Belgian. I've never been to Belgium, and I'm beginning to think I'll never leave here, but I don't think the towns over there can all look like ours. When people arrive in Léopoldville—and there are more and more of them these days thanks to all the factories sprouting up—they have a hard time getting their bearings to begin with. All the roads stick out, ramrod-straight, from little roundabouts, a bit like the Place de l'Étoile in Paris, except there's no Arc de Triomphe, and at the end of every avenue there's another little roundabout, and so on and so on, to the point where it can feel like one of those nightmares where you're walking in an endless maze. You find your way eventually, mind, thanks to the railway, the Seine and the church, but it's not easy, that's for sure.

Our neighbourhood's on the other side of the railway tracks, and the famous Belgian certainly didn't lay out the street plan round there. It's all stunted little houses, lined up any old how on a plain surrounded by chimney stacks spewing out great clouds of smoke that seem to stretch up into the sky for ever before falling back down on the town below. An ugly place, if you ask me. But it can't be all that bad, because once a painter set himself up with his palette behind our garden to paint the view. He came back day after day. I'd go and have a peek at his canvas each evening on the way back

7

from work. On his easel, the view looked even sadder to me. There was something disturbing about it, even—like one of those pauper's funerals not a soul turns up to. I was hoping he was going to add some sunshine to it, to brighten it up a bit, because honestly I couldn't see anyone wanting to hang that painting on their living-room wall. But one day the artist didn't come back. Instead of adding a bit of light to the top of his picture, he'd made do with adding his signature at the bottom, and I cried, thinking of all the sunshine he could've given us, but which he'd chosen to deny us instead, just like the Lord himself.

But listen to me going on… Does any of this matter at all? Well, yes, it does to me, because I'd like so much to make you understand why and how everything happened.

People are always saying you should grow to love the town you're brought up in, but you can tell that's not the case for me. I always hated Léopoldville, probably because I always saw it as it really was: artificial and sad. Towns shouldn't be built all in one go, by one man—they end up looking too much like warrens, and the people living there like rabbits.

Our house is the farthest out of the whole town, right next to the vegetable plots the factories have spared. They stretch all the way to the motorway, full of leeks, carrots or cabbages, depending on the year… We dread the cabbage years in our house because the whole place ends up stinking like gone-off sauerkraut. It doesn't matter if we keep the windows shut, the smell still gets in. I love the countryside, but I can't stand the farmers down that way, because they're not proper, simple country people, with their tractors and their jeans, and their leather boots from the Paris surplus stores. They're always off to the races on Sundays in their new cars, and their wives have got their own cars too… It's crazy what you can sell a leek for if you grow it just outside Paris.

Getting back to our place, though, it's a bit of a ruin if I'm honest. It's an old house, built long before the town sprouted up around it, and the walls are crumbling like nobody's business. Mum sometimes writes to the owners asking to get some repairs done, but they're having none of it. They inherited the place from an old uncle, and the family don't get along with each other so they won't even reply to our letters.

I know Mum could take them to court, only we're often behind with our rent, especially when Arthur—that's her man, my step-dad you might say—is on the dole, or on one of his benders.

I never knew my real dad, and I don't think Mum would recognize him either. She met him seventeen years ago at a dance. She reckons he must've been Italian, or something like that, and actually I do have dark hair. The tango, that's their speciality, the Italians, everyone says so. Mum must've had a bit too much to drink by the end of the night. They went and got frisky in the fields, and maybe that's why she still can't stand the smell of cabbage in the evening now.

When I came into the world, she put me with her mother, on the other side of the Seine, where all the quarries are. I lived there till I was six, then Granny died and I came to Léopoldville, to Arthur's house. I'd like to tell you about him, but there's not a lot to say. He's the sort of man who's always at the back of a group photo, with half his face hidden by some fat git spreading himself out. You know—the humble, timid type. Like a lot of weak blokes, he drinks to stiffen his nerve, and when he's had a few he'll mouth off at people he's usually polite to. Which explains why he's so often out of work.

It'll be fifteen years soon that Mum and Arthur've been together. They've never had a kid. I think Arthur would have liked at least one of his own, but Mum wasn't interested. I reckon they'll get married one day; Mum doesn't realize it, but Arthur's getting bourgeois tastes as he gets older, especially since he got the telly put in to get one over on the neighbours.

Before it all happened, I worked in a factory. It honestly wouldn't ever have occurred to me to work as a maid.

You can't get maids for love nor money round here. The proof is that the doctors and the managers get theirs shipped in from Brittany. They put adverts in the local papers in Morbihan or Finistère, and up turn a load of dumpy, rosy-cheeked girls, carrying brand-new cardboard suitcases. They stay in the job for a couple of months, time for them to settle in and lose their healthy complexions; then they quit and go and work at the factory, because the pay's better and after six o'clock you're free to do what you like.

But it was just that freedom that got to me! Every day that sad road, with the stream of moped riders shouting filthy things at you... The level crossing with the crowd of workers up against it, with their dirty, wandering hands... And then Arthur's ramshackle, barely furnished house... Arthur himself, lanky, dull as a turnip, with his jutting chin, his wispy little moustache, his lips spotted with flecks of cigarette paper.

No, I swear, I just couldn't take it any more.

I started by changing my routine. To get home, I'd go through the centre of Léopoldville instead. It's just as sad a place as the rest of the town, but at least you can feel the money round there. The houses are built from limestone and set in the middle of lawns, where sprinklers turn and spray in the evenings.

And that's how I first saw the Roolands' house.

TWO

At first sight, it looked like the others: two storeys, an arrow-shaped weathervane sitting on top of the gable roof, with little stained-glass windows and some steps leading up to a front door flanked by light-blue earthenware pots... But what set it apart was a funny sort of feeling that floated in the air around the house. How can I explain it? It seemed like it was *somewhere else*. Yes, it was a Léopoldville house, but it existed on a sort of desert island all of its own. A tiny, mysterious island, and one where the natives seemed to live bloody well too.

On the red-sand driveway sat a magnificent green American car, its polished chrome gleaming, with white upholstery that reminded me of a living room I'd seen once, from the over-ground Métro in Paris... I'd only caught sight of it for a couple of seconds, but I'd dreamt of that living room ever since. In my mind, sinking back into a big white leather armchair seemed like the greatest happiness the world had to offer.

The garden stretched in front of the house, a little carpet of green lawn, in the middle of which sat a marvellous swing seat, scattered with cushions and sheltered by a blue canopy. That seat looked like happiness to me too. Monsieur and Madame Rooland would relax there at dusk, glasses of whisky resting next to them on stands like iron tulips, while a wireless with a great big aerial played jazz music. I can't tell you how enchanting the atmosphere of that garden was, with the beautiful, shining car, that music, those drinks that you could just tell were so wonderfully chilled, and that couple, gently swinging while the seat creaked.

At first I contented myself with just slowing down as I went past the front of the house. Later, I was so completely captivated that I started going back and forth in front of the place. Round there they called them "the Yanks".

He had an average build, reddish-brown hair, with splashes of coppery freckles on his face and arms. He looked around thirty-five and worked at NATO headquarters in Rocquencourt. When he went out he'd wear a light suit of charcoal brown or fawn, with an open-collared white shirt and a black straw hat, jazzed up with a black-and-white-checked ribbon. At home in the evenings, though, he'd just wear grey cotton trousers and a loud shirt—one time, I remember, he wore one covered in palm trees and sand dunes. On anyone else that shirt would have seemed corny, but Monsieur Rooland had the class to pull it off. His wife was a different sort altogether. She was younger than him, but somehow she almost seemed the older of the pair. A brunette, with flecks of sunlight in her hair, she was always wearing a pair of coral-pink shorts and a light-green blouse. She had rosy skin, and I don't know why but I got it into my head that she must have Red Indian blood. She was a chain-smoker and rolled her shoulders when she walked, like a long-jumper taking a run-up.

Eventually they noticed what I was up to. A French couple would have taken offence, I'm sure. Or at least they would have wanted to know what I was after, why I was there outside their house at six every day, like a kid with my nose pressed up against a shop window. But the Roolands found it funny more than anything else. They started smiling at me as I went by and then, one evening, maybe after he'd had a few whiskies, Monsieur Rooland called out in English, "Hello!", and gave me a little wave of his hand. I felt my heart burst into flame.

I can't tell you how the idea came to me. Do you know what I reckon a thought is? It's like a flash of sunlight that dazzles you without you knowing where it came from.

But one evening, as I arrived back at Arthur's, I realized that the sun only truly shone at the Roolands'.

Like I was telling you, it was a desert island all to itself! An island like you see on the holiday-company adverts, all flowers, the easy life and cool drinks within arm's reach. Life on a swing.

On that particular evening, Arthur was rat-arsed. He's always had two types of pissed: wine-pissed and rum-pissed. Wine makes him merry, but rum—that just makes him nasty. That day he'd downed half a bottle of Negrita, and you could see in his eyes that he'd decided not to spare anyone.

"You're late again!" he said, straight off.

He was sitting in front of the telly. I've never seen anything more depressing than that TV—it's alone in a room with just three chairs stupidly lined up in front of it. There was nothing on yet. The screen was just a weirdly flickering white fog, but Arthur didn't even seem to have noticed.

"I've come from the factory," I said, taking off my shoes.

"And what way do you take back from the factory, my dear? Did you take the scenic route?"

"I take whatever route I please!"

It'd been years since he'd hit me. Arthur's not really the type for a slap, I'll give him that. That evening, though, it went off. Mum was just getting back from the grocer's, and she heard the wallop all the way from the kitchen. She came running and

15

saw the mark of her man's hand on my face. I was stunned, crying without even realizing it.

"What did she do?"

I haven't told you about Mum yet. I'm a bit embarrassed by it. She's got what they call a harelip. Along with me, that's what messed her life up. I reckon it must have been because of the lip thing that my dad, the Italian from the dance, never showed his face again after their fumble in the cabbage fields. If they'd stitched her lip up properly when she was a kid it would have changed her whole universe. She could probably have found a better bloke than Arthur, because apart from her lip she's not bad—petite, but with all the curves in the right places to please a man.

The slap had hurt Arthur more than me. He was standing there like an idiot in front of the blank screen, his arm hanging by his side, fingers twitching, but he tried to save some dignity:

"She spoke to me like the insolent girl she is!"

And then he added:

"She reads too much, it's turning her head!"

That was his hobbyhorse, my reading. He couldn't get his head round the idea that they'd print anything other than the Communist Party rag. One day, after a rum session, he'd torn up two books I'd borrowed from the library, which caused a right load of bother when it turned out they were out-of-print editions. Since then, I'd started buying my own books and reselling them to the second-hand dealers by the Seine when I went up to Paris.

Mum sighed. I put on my shoes and left. Honestly, the air in that house was unbreathable; the air in the whole area was. It was a grey evening out. Disgusting smells came wafting on the wind, not just from the cabbage fields, but from the chemical plant too. The skyline was all factory chimneys and building sites.

Those new houses frightened me a bit. This fresh town, sprouting up so quickly, these outsiders coming to rob us of the small amount of charm Léopoldville had to offer—I had a bad feeling about all of it.

I started running. The level-crossing barrier was down and I pushed open the gate. The station was a hundred metres away. A train sat by the platform, panting in a cloud of steam. The crossing guard shouted something, and then I saw the express from Caen bearing down on me. I just had time to throw myself out of the way… I was shaken up. They're right to put those warning signs up in the stations: *One train may hide another.*

La Magnin was a fat, jaundiced woman who panted every time she turned the crank to shift the barrier.

"Can't you look before you—"

I carried on running. And I knew where I was going.

When I got to the Roolands' house they weren't on their blue swing any more. They were having their dinner on a folding table set out in front of the porch. They were the only ones in Léopoldville who dared to eat like that, in the open air, in plain sight of all and sundry. They couldn't have cared less about being watched.

I pushed open the gate and walked up the red-sand drive. I saw the car up close for the first time. It was even more beautiful than it looked from a distance. The paintwork gleamed, and it had a smell like you can't describe. It smelt of wealth, of power.

I was walking in a trance. If you could have seen me! My head straight up like a soldier on parade, my arms stiff by my sides, my whole being filled up with my heart, which was pounding fit to burst.

Madame Rooland was eating with her left arm resting on her knee in a funny pose. Her husband was opening a couple of cartons of fruit juice. He stopped when he saw me come out from behind the car. I froze too. I looked at the table. I was a prize idiot to have set foot on this island. Instead of eating from plates like the rest of us, they each had a tray in front of them with beans in brown sauce, salad, tomatoes and meat covered in a sort of pink jelly.

The woman smiled at me without getting up. He poked two straws through the triangular holes he'd just punched in the cartons with a special sort of tool.

"Hello, Mademoiselle!"

He was glowing. It was the splashes of red freckles that did it—sort of like dull fire burning on his skin. His eyes seemed lighter than they had from far away. I had to explain myself but I was too overcome with emotion. Instead of pressing me, they waited. Madame Rooland finished chewing her mouthful and he sucked on a straw.

"I'm sorry for bothering you…"

"You're not bothering us," he assured me. "Would you like an *orange juice*?"

These last words were in English, but I realized he was offering me a fruit juice and I was gobsmacked.

I march into their garden like a lunatic, and instead of asking me what I'm playing at, here they are offering me a drink!

"No, thank you."

He had a wonderful smile, Monsieur Rooland. Teeth even whiter than in the cinema commercials, a deep dimple in his chin.

"I came to ask whether you needed a maid."

His smile shrank a little, but his teeth still shone in the twilight. Madame Rooland asked him a question in American. She didn't understand French perfectly, and I felt it was the word "maid" she hadn't got. Her husband explained; she looked at me. This time it was the look any woman gives a young girl who's just offered her services.

"You're a servant?"

"No, I work in a factory."

"And you've lost your job?"

"No."

I swear I shocked him with that, smooth American though he was.

"So, why?" he murmured.

I knew I had to get my ideas in order, explain myself... But it wasn't easy.

"I'm not happy!"

Hearing myself say that, I blushed in confusion.

"How old are you?"

"Seventeen and a half."

"And you're unhappy! I know people in my country who'd give four hundred million dollars to be your age."

I felt a surge of boldness:

"Introduce them to me, then. I'm ready to discuss the matter!"

I've never seen a man laugh so hard. He was in tears, slapping his thighs. Then suddenly he stopped and asked:

"Why do you want to be a maid here?"

"Because I like this place," I mumbled, looking around me.

The woman said something in her language. Judging by her tone, it wasn't positive...

"Doesn't Madame Rooland like the idea?" I blurted.

"She says she doesn't need anyone... She's already a little bored in this country..."

"A lot!" corrected Madame Rooland.

"...and if she didn't have to look after the house any more she'd be bored to death," her husband finished, ignoring her interruption.

"If I worked with her it'd be less boring. It's different when there's two of you," I replied.

I imagine when you're in the dock, in court, you must feel like I did then: desperate to justify yourself, to say anything at all just to prove you're good at heart.

I looked through one of the open windows. The house was in a state. If that was what Madame Rooland called doing the housework then I hadn't arrived a second too soon! I could hardly say that, though. She wouldn't have been best pleased. When I'd passed by the house on the pavement and looked at them both in the shade of their swing, she'd seemed gentle to me, somehow. Strangely gentle in a way that I'd put down to her "Indian blood" at the time. But by now I could tell she wasn't as easy-going as all that.

She'd started eating again, her left arm still resting on her knees.

"All right," I sighed, "I'm sorry..."

I couldn't keep on at them. I gave them the least sad smile that I could, and left. The sand squeaked quietly beneath my feet. And you will never know how big that green car seemed, or how deliciously it smelt of America.

THREE

I cried my eyes out that evening in my shabby little bedroom. It had been decided, apparently: I would always be a prisoner in Léopoldville. The factory, men groggy from wine and fatigue, the bitter stench of cabbages and a television screen with me, Mum and Arthur forever lined up in front of it on our rickety chairs—that was all the future held for me.

The next day, at Ridel's factory I did my work in a daze, automatically. It wasn't anything complicated. I was on the assembly line: car seats. My job was "trimmings", stitching plastic rims onto the edges. At six o'clock I felt the urge to go home via the Roolands', but I resisted. From now on, my route would be that of the level crossing and the crowd of factory workers, their mopeds spewing bluish clouds of exhaust smoke, the sound of their backfiring engines drilling through my skull.

I got home earlier than usual. And then, would you believe, my heart near enough leapt out of my chest.

Monsieur Rooland's car was parked in front of our house. It took up practically the whole street. As I passed I gave a clip round the ear to one of the Coindets' kids, who was trying to write "shit" in the dust on the beautiful bodywork.

I burst into our place like a lunatic. Monsieur Rooland was there, sat on the best chair (an old one with turned legs that we got from Granny), his hat on the back of his head. Mum was standing in front of him, looking awkward as anything. She takes good care of herself normally, but it was a Friday, washing day, so she was wearing a scruffy old shirt, an old rag tied round her waist like an apron. Classy! I was ashamed of the bubbling washing pot, slopping all over the stove top, ashamed of the poxy furniture, of our fly-shit-covered lampshade with its pearl tassels and—I admit it—ashamed of Mum's harelip.

"Look, here she is!" she said.

And straight off, her voice trembling with indignation, she asked:

"What's all this I hear, Louise? Did you go offering your services to these people?"

"Yes."

"Why didn't you tell me?"

I shrugged. Monsieur Rooland gave an embarrassed smile. I took it out on him to hide my shame.

"How did you know where I lived?"

"The man in the tobacconist's opposite my place told me who you were…"

"Why did you come?"

"Because we've thought it over, my wife and I. We'd like to take you on."

And then it was as if nothing else mattered. I don't know if you know how it feels, you lot, to be really, properly happy, happy all over. It was like I was sinking into an ocean of warmth and light…

"You're taking me on?"

"If you're still interested, yes."

His accent was like music. Or at least, like the kind of music he played on his wireless with the big aerial.

"Louise, you're crazy! You've got a good position at Ridel's. They like you there."

She wasn't going to let herself be dazzled by the beautiful car or the black straw hat. She had her feet on the ground, as she said. It was no glamorous job being a maid, and where would it get me, working for Americans? They'd go back home sooner or later and I'd be out on the street.

Only I didn't see it that way. Quite the opposite: I could already see myself leaving with them, on board the *Liberty*, going to shine their shoes in America.

"I want to go, Mum!"

I'd never spoken to her in that tone before. She twisted the cloth of her makeshift apron, her hand raw and wrinkled from the washing. She wanted to slap me, I could tell. How she managed to keep control of herself I still wonder. Now, after everything that's happened, I reckon if she'd given me the back of her hand at that moment it would have been the best thing she'd ever done.

I turned to Monsieur Rooland. He'd rolled up the sleeves of his sports jacket, as if it were just a shirt. He had a fat gold watch on his wrist, but it shone less brightly than his patches of freckles.

"Say something, Monsieur Rooland!" I begged.

He was American, so he said just what an American would say in a situation like that:

"How much do you earn at the factory?"

Mum got in first.

"Thirty thousand francs."

It wasn't true. At least, not entirely. I got thirty thousand during the motor show when we were working flat out and there was overtime to burn, but normally I'd only bring home twenty-two to twenty-five thousand a month.

He took a cigarette from his pocket. I think it was the way he lit it, more than anything else, that won Mum over. He struck the match on the heel of his shoe. Just a little scrape and it blazed into life. You could try all your life and you'd never manage it.

"I'll give her thirty thousand and her meals. OK?"

Mum didn't know what else to say.

"You know," I ventured, "I could always go back to the factory if things didn't work out…"

And that's how it came about. Mum shrugged in agreement, and sighed:

"What'll Arthur say, I wonder."

She was right—it was a bit harder with him.

As I said, he's a bit of a Communist, Arthur. On the leaflets he used to bring home there were always big headlines ranting about Americans lynching blacks and exploiting workers and calling them warmongers. I never really knew what a "monger" was, and I don't think Arthur did either, but he'd shout it at the top of his voice as if he'd invented the word.

When we told him the news he hit the roof, saying if I was going to go to the Yanks' I'd never set foot in his house again, and much worse besides, but he was sober, and a weak bloke like him was never going to be a match for two determined women without a glass of wine or two inside him. He gave in in the end because there was a wrestling match on the telly (the Béthune Bruiser versus Doctor Kaiser) and he couldn't bear to miss it.

The next day, I went and picked up my final pay packet from Ridel's. Monsieur Rooland had told me his wife would wait for me all day. I just stopped by to drop off my pay at home, and get a smile from Mum in return, and then I went straight over to the Americans'. I felt like I was on my way to New York! And when I saw Madame Rooland standing on her front step I almost wondered whether it was the Statue of Liberty.

FOUR

I still ask myself, whose role is more embarrassing in a situation like that—the servant who's never been a servant before or the mistress who's never been a mistress?

Madame Rooland looked me up and down for a good long moment—not so much with a critical eye, more like she was trying to think of what she should say. Eventually, she nodded:

"Come and see the house."

I went to the palace at Versailles with school once. We had a one-armed tour guide who reeked of cheap wine, like Arthur after one of his merrier piss-ups. His heels rang out on the kings' polished wood floors as he proclaimed:

"This is the Queen's room. It is here that she gave birth to…"

And I imagined the queens all giving birth to little princes. It made me come over all strange. Well, when Madame Rooland announced: "This is our bedchamber" (she spoke French like that: I always had to keep myself from laughing at her funny little turns of phrase) it made me imagine her with her husband, in all sorts of poses that a young girl shouldn't know about. You wouldn't believe the shapes they twisted themselves into.

The headboard was padded, as were the wardrobe doors. There were chairs, and rugs scattered all over the floor, but nothing on the walls: no paintings, no ornaments… Dirty laundry was piling up in the corners. She was a slattern, Madame Rooland: always spick and span herself, in her green blouse, her orange lipstick and her classy hairdo, but lazy like you wouldn't believe when it came to the housework.

She showed me all the rooms. There were nine in all, five of which were unused. As we looked around, a question occurred to me, but I didn't dare ask. When we'd finished, it came out all of its own:

"And my bedroom?" I murmured.

She stared at me, shocked. She looked almost like a little girl.

"Your bedroom?"

"Yes! A maid should sleep in the house, they have to… I've got to make breakfast in the morning, haven't I?"

"But… But you don't live far away."

"That doesn't matter. Suppose you need something in the night?"

A scene from an American movie came helpfully to mind.

"Look, suppose you want a glass of milk, for example. You just call me and I go and get it for you."

"Oh, I see! Very well, choose whichever room you want."

"Any of them?"

"Of course, it is not importance."

I felt as if a good fairy had taken me by the hand and led me into a fantastical toy shop. Choose! It was too tempting. Cheekily, I chose the best room there was. It was near theirs. Only the bathroom was in between. He'd rented the house furnished, Monsieur Rooland, and only bought furniture for their bedroom and the garden. There was no padded headboard in my room—just a normal bed with marquetry inlay and a red eiderdown, a mahogany dresser, a round table covered with a lace cloth. A pair of wicker chairs and a leather armchair completed the set-up. You get the idea.

"I'll go and get my things this afternoon if that's all right?"

"OK!"

We went back downstairs. What a place to live! It felt as if I'd left Léopoldville and been transported to some faraway country.

"What's your name?" asked Madame Rooland.

"Louise Lacroix, Madame."

"Don't call me Madame—call me Thelma."

"What?"

In a flash I saw my old boss, Ridel. His first name was Lucien. He was a big deal and not half self-important with it. I think he'd have liked us all to believe the good Lord called him up every morning to ask his permission to let the Earth go round the sun. I imagined his face if I'd had the nerve to call him Lucien!

"Why are you laughing, Louise? Isn't it a nice name, Thelma?"

"Oh, yes, Madame, it's just that maids don't call their employers by their first names."

"Well what do they call them?"

"Madame!"

"Just 'Madame'?"

"Yes."

"OK."

With that she lit a cigarette, and offered me her packet of Camels.

"No, thank you, I don't smoke… Where would you like me to start, Madame?"

She answered in her own language by mistake. Seeing that I didn't understand, she translated for me:

"It is not importance."

She seemed somehow sad all of a sudden. I could tell I was in the way a bit. She was going to have to get used to having me around, and that small effort annoyed her. I was going to have to pull out all the stops to win her over.

"It's almost eleven. Does Monsieur Rooland come home for lunch?"

"No."

"And you, do you have a big meal at lunchtime?"

"No… I am just drink a tea with toast."

Was she watching her figure or was that just how they did things here? Lunch at ours was more like a plate of lentils and sausages, or a mutton stew. I've never been mad about tea.

"Me too, Madame, if that's all right."

I took a plastic apron from the kitchen and got to work. It was just laziness on her part, all that mess. There was everything you needed to clean a house there: vacuum cleaner, floor polisher, washing machine and a load of other gadgets that I didn't really understand the point of.

I started by washing the pile of dirty dishes, then by cleaning the top of the electric cooker, which was filthy with stains from pots that had boiled over. Then I went over the tiled floor with a broom. When my kitchen was clean, I started on the bathroom. Talk about a bomb site! A cat could have lost her kittens in there. Dirty laundry, lipstick crushed on the floor, hairs in the bath, combs sticking out of the soap, towels hanging off the shower head and the bath taps. You could tell the furnishings weren't hers! She was letting everything go to pot.

I worked for hours. From time to time Madame Rooland came and watched, looking at me like I wasn't all there. Always with a cigarette in her gob and an American paperback in her hand with some awful picture on the cover (a horror story, I reckoned).

By four, everything was finished, shining, neat and orderly… It was a different sort of house altogether.

"May I go and get my suitcase, Madame?"

"Yes."

"Since I'm going out, perhaps I could do the shopping for this evening?"

"There's no need, we've plenty of food in the kitchen."

I'd seen. Tins! Tins, of all colours, shapes and sizes. The Roolands ate nothing else, it seemed—perhaps just buying enough fruit and salad to keep the scurvy away. But my afternoon's work had pepped me up.

"In France we save tins for picnics, Madame… Or we eat them when there's no time to cook from scratch."

"What is it signify, 'cook from scratch'?"

"To prepare a meal. Since I have time, I'll cook for you, if you don't mind?"

You'd have to hear it to believe it, the way she used to say "OK!" As if she was holding her nose.

"Do you have any preferences?"

"No!"

I was expecting her to give me some money for the shopping, but she was so taken aback that it didn't occur to her, so I set off, telling myself that Mum had left me a couple of thousand francs from my last pay packet, and it wouldn't hurt to give a little loan to my new employers.

*

When I got home Mum was sitting next to the window, darning a pair of Arthur's boxers. The blood drained from her face when she saw me.

"I knew it! You're not up to it, you little idiot."

She really thought I'd got myself sacked by the Roolands already.

"Not at all, Mum, it's all going like a dream. I do just as I like…"

I told her about my day. She sighed.

"They're a funny old couple all right. And they let you come and go like this?"

"I've come to get my things."

"What do you mean?"

"What do you think? Maids live in."

"But there was no mention of that…"

"Not the other day, no. But this morning there was! Madame Rooland even wants me to sleep in a room near hers. She has medication she needs to take at night."

When I was little, my mum convinced me that my nose twitched whenever I lied. That it was a dead giveaway. From then on, if I was telling her porkies, she only had to glance at the end of my nose and, without thinking, I'd move my hand to cover it, giving myself away. This time I restrained myself.

"So, you're leaving us completely."

"Don't be daft, Mum—I'll be five minutes away!"

"Well, I haven't heard the last of Arthur's grumbling, then."

"He's not my dad, Mum…"

The smell of cabbages had never been so strong. Mum went back to her darning.

In a quarter of an hour, my packing was done. As wardrobes go, mine wasn't huge, and I didn't want to take everything in case it gave Mum the impression I was leaving for good. Back in the kitchen, I asked:

"Mum, do you reckon I could pick some flowers from the garden for the boss?"

"Go on, then."

The soil in our garden's black. It doesn't stick together in great clods like it would in the real countryside. Instead, it crumbles into a fine dust under your spade. Everything that grows in it has the same look: somehow shrivelled and stunted, withered before it even has a chance to bloom. Or maybe I'm imagining it—people round here seem to think it's normal enough, the way things are.

Picking some of Arthur's marigolds and dahlias, I heard the pigeons cooing in the loft he'd built next to the toilet. Pigeons, telly and booze—they're his vices. He's got four pairs, each pair in their own little box house. White, they are, with sort of curly wing tips.

I remembered that the pair on the end had some little ones that were just about ready for the pot. The evening before, Arthur had been talking about having them the Sunday coming. I had an idea. I ran and shouted to Mum.

"Mum, would you come and wring the necks of these little pigeons for me?"

"You're not serious?"

"It's for the Roolands!"

She really let me have it then. All the bitterness she had brewing inside her came right out in my face. She'd had it up to here with those Americans. They were taking everything

33

from her and Arthur already, and now they were supposed to shower them with flowers and food too?

I looked guiltily at Arthur's flower bed—just a patch of stubble now. I let the storm blow itself out. Mum's harelip had turned purple. When she ran out of breath, I took my chance.

"Just listen, would you, instead of going off on one? I'll pay for them. A good price too! I was just trying to do Arthur a good turn."

She didn't only kill the birds, squeezing them under their wings, she plucked and gutted them for me too. I returned "home" in triumph, having picked up some fatty bacon and peas on the way as well. I'd never been much of a cook. There was certainly nothing fancy about what I ate at home with Mum and Arthur. But that hadn't stopped me reading the recipes in women's magazines. (Some of which even had colour illustrations!)

And the recipe for *pigeon flambé sur canapé* was engraved on my memory...

FIVE

Monsieur Rooland got a shock when he came home, that's for sure. I'd laid the cutlery for dinner out on a tablecloth (there was no actual tablecloth, but I'd made do with a couple of tea towels) and not straight onto the bare table like Madame Rooland had always done before me. There was a bunch of marigolds in a jar too, which brightened things up, and the smell coming from the kitchen… well, it was mouth-watering, even if I do say so myself. Monsieur Rooland asked his wife something in American. I think she must have told him that everything had gone well, because he gave me one of his water-skiing-commercial smiles.

He washed his hands while his wife made them a couple of whiskies, then they went and sat in their swing seat under the blue canopy and talked about me for a while.

Half an hour later, I went and got changed to serve them dinner. I still had a black dress that I'd bought for an uncle's funeral. When I tied an apron on top of it I looked like a real maid. The only apron I had was pink, but then that was more cheerful in a way.

And so I took them out my two pigeons, beautifully golden, draped with slices of bacon, all sitting on a bed of croutons. Now for the big moment—confidently, I grabbed the whisky bottle, glugged a measure over my two little birds, struck a match and—*woosh*! Ah, if you could have seen those flames leaping, and the Roolands' stunned faces! I swear, there are people with the Legion of Honour who've done less for the glory of France than I did that day.

They asked me to sit with them, but I refused. Everyone has their place. Mine was in the kitchen. I was washing the dishes as I served so as not to let it all get on top of me. What I wanted above all was to show them that, in a bright, happy house like theirs, everything should always be kept clean and neat. When they came inside, after God knows how many cigarettes, night had fallen. There was a glow in the sky over towards the factories, and insects zigzagged through the garden air, attracted by a nearby street lamp. The car's chrome bumpers shone in its white light. Now that my work was over and I could feel the tiredness in my limbs I would have loved for Monsieur Rooland to take me out for a spin.

I would have sat in the front, next to the driver, looking at all the dials on the dashboard. When it was running, the car made so little noise that you couldn't even hear it coming. And there was the radio, of course. Yes, I could imagine myself leaning back on that white leather, soft music in my ears, watching Monsieur Rooland's freckled hands on the steering wheel.

"Louise!"

He was standing behind me. He'd caught me looking at the car from the kitchen window.

"Yes, Monsieur?"

"I just wanted to say, well done. My wife and I are very pleased."

"Thank you, Monsieur. Me too."

He came a little closer, to see what I'd been looking at. Until then, men had always scared me a bit. If I was sure you wouldn't laugh at me, I'd tell you why… Well, all right: it was because of their feet. Plenty of nice-looking boys had tried chatting me up, and I'd known some who could have charmed the birds from the trees with their patter. It's crazy how cocky and confident the kids are round our way. There were times when their compliments, their fresh smiles, their eyes which seem to kiss you with a glance... There were times when all that had got to me. But the moment always came when I looked down at their feet and a strange sort of fear would take hold of me. I realized they were nothing but animals. The more I think about it, I reckon this fear of feet must come from my granddad. I was four when he died. They kept me away from the deathbed, but when they came to put him in the coffin with all the family gathered round in tears, I managed to sneak up close to take a look, and what shocked me, what scared me, wasn't his white hands clutched tight around a rosary, wasn't his pinched, waxy face, it was his big postman's feet in his Sunday shoes, showing me their soles for the first time.

Since then, men's feet had terrified me. When a boy was kissing me, if I thought about his two shoes, flat on the ground in front of mine, I'd push him away as hard as I could and run. The kids round my way started saying I wasn't right in the head, leaving only the new arrivals to flirt with me a bit. But a reputation's a reputation and it never went very far.

"Do you want to go back home to sleep, Louise?"

"No, Monsieur."

Monsieur Rooland's feet didn't scare me at all. They seemed neat and peaceful to me in their canvas sandals. Maybe because they were small? Maybe because they were tanned? Maybe because they were American feet too? Who knows what really goes on, down in the depths of your brain? Anyway, for the first time in my life I'd met a pair of feet that felt normal to me.

"But Louise," he insisted, "you were looking so sadly out of the window. If you want to go home, you must say so."

"I don't want to go home, I'm very happy here, Monsieur. I was just looking at your car, Monsieur. Admiring it."

He looked too.

"It's a Dodge," he said. As if that explained something.

In the shadows it looked like a slumbering monster.

"It's beautiful. I've never seen a car like it."

He took my chin in his hand to look me in the face. His eyes were laughing.

"You want to go for a ride, don't you?"

I looked away, but nodded.

"OK, come on."

And off we went, just like that. Monsieur Rooland shouted to his wife that we'd be back, and Thelma didn't ask any questions. Apparently, it seemed totally normal to her that her husband would take the maid for a ride at nine o'clock in the evening, him in short sleeves and the servant wearing an apron.

He opened the gate. I stayed next to the passenger door—not daring, not knowing how, to open it.

"Get in!"

You had to push a little catch on the door handle with your thumb. He showed me how. It was easy. You wouldn't believe how heavy the door was! A safe door couldn't have been any heavier.

Inside the car, it was even better than I'd imagined. The smell, more than anything: leather, perfume, the powerful engine. The windscreen had a slight blue tint to it. You couldn't see it from the outside, but once you were inside the car that curved window would add a touch of beauty to even the most depressing landscapes. He put the radio on, just as I'd dreamt, and the music that burst into life came from everywhere at once, as if we were sitting inside a loudspeaker rather than a car.

"Everything all right?" asked Monsieur Rooland.

I croaked a "yes", which made him snort with laughter. He drove right across Léopoldville in a matter of seconds: our little town that I thought was a sprawl. As if! We took the straight road lined with double rows of trees that leads down to the Seine. I didn't recognize the surroundings any more. The car transformed them. We drove slowly up the old towpath leading to the lock, its red lamps leaving long purple smears on the surface of the river.

The barges moored up at the banks for the night were like a daisy chain of fainter lights.

"All right?"

Why did he feel the need to talk to me? And why on earth keep repeating that stupid question? Of course it was all right! It was wonderful in his car. I remember the radio was playing an arrangement of "Que Sera, Sera". Everything was how I'd imagined it. Tiny red and green lights were blinking on the dashboard, Monsieur Rooland's hands caressed the steering wheel, while his feet—his feet that didn't scare me one bit—danced on the pedals.

At the lock we took the bumpy road that leads back to the factories, hazel branches lashing at the car roof.

Ten minutes later we were back at their house.

*

Madame Rooland had changed. Instead of her shorts and blouse, she was wearing a white terry-cloth dressing gown with yellow and green stripes, and it wasn't hard to tell that she had nothing else on underneath. She was sprawled on the living room sofa, one leg in the air. On the floor an automatic turntable was playing Elvis Presley's "Loving You".

"Hello!" was all she said, in English.

All of a sudden I got the impression that she wasn't herself any more—that she'd changed somehow while we'd been out. I caught a glance of the whisky bottle sitting next to the sofa and understood. Thelma had drunk a good third of it. With that, I understood the state of the house, and her reluctance to have someone at home with her all day. Maybe she missed America? Her husband must have used all his charm to get her to agree to take me on. He probably hoped I'd be a good influence.

He went and sat down next to her. She grabbed the bottle clumsily.

"Pour a glass for my husband, Louise!"

When I came back from the kitchen with the glass she was lying across the sofa, pawing at Monsieur Rooland: "Jess, Jess." It was enough to make anyone blush. I tried to make myself scarce, but she called me back.

"No, Louise! Have a drink with us."

"I don't drink, Madame."

"Just *one*, to make me happy…"

So I went to the kitchen to get another glass. When I came back again, Jess had managed to get away from her. He was at the other end of the room, next to the fireplace, his glass in his hand. He looked unhappy—I'd not seen him like that before.

He put his whisky down on the black marble mantelpiece, next to the clock stuck on six o'clock, and came to take my glass.

"Just a little drop, Monsieur Rooland."

Thelma's dressing gown had fallen open, putting everything on display that a lady would normally keep to herself. Her eyes were shining and she was laughing strangely, her lips drawn back like a dog about to bite.

She was saying things I didn't understand, and which seemed to be annoying her husband.

"Chin-chin, Louise," he said abruptly.

I took a sip. It was so strong it burned my throat. How on earth could she drink it?

"You don't like it?"

"No, Monsieur. Excuse me—may I go to bed?"

"Of course, Louise."

Well there you go—what a mess life is. On my first evening at the Roolands', instead of dancing for joy I cried.

All because of the look Jess gave me when I said goodnight—a look that seemed to express all the unhappiness of men.

SIX

She kept a lid on it for a few more days. (When I say she kept a lid on it, I mean she waited until dinner to start boozing.) But then what little willpower she had gave way. I walked in on her one morning to see her knocking back a glass of Scotch right after her first Camel of the day. She did absolutely nothing apart from drink and listen to records. Her red face had nothing to do with any Indian blood—it was the booze! She reminded me of Arthur when he was on a Negrita binge and his pasty face would turn purple.

I'd often played "Loving You" on the jukebox in the café where I'd go for a drink with my factory mates during the cinema interval on Saturday nights. I loved Presley's throaty voice. I don't know why, but I told myself he must have nice feet… Anyway, pretty soon I was sick of that song. It wasn't the record player playing it really, it was a bottle of whisky!

Thelma dragged herself from the garden to the living room, and from the living room to the bedroom. She'd take several showers throughout the day—not to keep clean, but to sober up. Then she'd start drinking again. All that took the wind right out of my sails. I'm sure you can imagine, it was hardly an encouraging start to my employment. But what made up for it was Monsieur Rooland. He came back every evening at five thirty sharp. He'd get changed, and then allow himself a couple of drinks under the blue canopy, so as to join his wife where she was floating, a few centimetres above the ground.

He seemed to enjoy the little dishes that I tried so hard to put together for him. As these Americans seemed to know nothing about food, I started inventing my own recipes once I'd gone through all the ones in the magazines. They liked everything, and especially anything with a sauce.

Over there, in their country, the sauces come in bottles and all taste the same. It's only the label on the bottle that changes, as I realized when sneaking a taste of some of their precious supplies from the cupboards.

Dinner was the best part of the day. I'd hide myself away in the kitchen and watch Jess eat from the window. He seemed more and more handsome to me every day, although if I'm honest he wasn't really all that good-looking. The girls from the factory wouldn't have found him to their taste, I'm sure. They wouldn't have appreciated that slightly sad, casual charm, those bright eyes, those coppery freckles or the blinding white smile he'd flash at me when he caught me watching him.

When I came to clear the table, he'd wink.

"That was OK, Louise."

I blushed every time. It felt like my face had been wrapped in a hot towel. After dinner they'd go to the living room, and from then on it was whisky, the record player and Madame Rooland pawing at her husband.

Often, Thelma would invent some reason to call me in. She wanted someone to watch—it excited her. I'd go and huddle at the end of the room, near the fireplace. *I'd* know how to make Jess happy, I told myself.

What with all Thelma's drunken antics, I was a lot less happy at the Roolands' than I'd expected. Having said that, I wasn't

44

unhappy either. When I think back to that time, I'm left with a sensation of the days flying by at great speed, each one exactly the same as the last—more so than at Arthur's, even. They were lined up one after the other, like pearls on a string. My housework, preparing dinner… Presley's voice, the glugging of whisky, the tinkling of the ice cubes that Thelma rolled expertly round her glass, making sure the sides were coated in alcohol. Sometimes she'd call me into her bedroom, to try on her clothes.

"I want to perceive elegance."

I let her do it. She draped me in dresses, pinched and pulled at blouses to take them in or loosen them, her thin hands lingering on my body. I stayed frozen, like a mannequin, not understanding what pleasure it could possibly give her to dress and undress me like that.

When she'd finished, her clothes would all be strewn across the bed.

"OK, Louise."

I went back downstairs, while she poured herself an even bigger glass than the others.

The hours I spent in her company were strange and depressing, but from the moment the Dodge was parked in the driveway everything changed. I burst into song. I liked Sundays just as much. Not all of them, as they went to Paris once a month to see some American friends, but on the other three Sundays in the month they would stay at home, and on those days the atmosphere was different. Technically it was a day off for me, but where better to spend it than in my new home? I'd lounge around in my bedroom, try on a dress, a blouse, put on a bit of make-up…

"Come and sit in the garden, Louise."

There was room for three on the swing seat. Thelma sat in the middle, with me clutching the armrest on my side very tightly—I've never liked swings. She hid Monsieur Rooland's body from me, but I could see his crossed legs and tell how muscular they were under his alpaca-wool trousers. His right heel dug into the grass as he pushed us back and forth. I'd lie back and let myself float in this dream, repeating to myself "I'm on the island! I'm on the desert island!" And I only had to look up at the clouds in the sky to find all the details missing from my surroundings: one of them was a palm tree, another a coral reef, and the blue of the sky was the sea. One day I even saw a cannibal, but this time he wasn't floating in the sky, he was standing in front of the garden gate, and he looked so much like Arthur that I felt myself going green at the gills.

Drunk Arthur. Mean Arthur. He cackled at the sight of me lounging next to the Yanks.

"Tart! Tart!"

He shook his fist at me. Monsieur Rooland got up to go and get rid of him, thinking that he was just some drunk or other, but I stopped him.

"No, leave him, he's my mum's man."

"Is he drunk?"

"Yes."

Jess Rooland was all too used to drunks. He sat down again.

Arthur was making a right old scene, his eyes wild, his mouth wet and glistening.

"Have you gone off your rocker?" I hissed, rushing over to him. "This isn't exactly good manners, is it?"

46

"You're a whore, Louise," he answered. "Hanging around these bastards like a little floozy. Nothing but a whore. My bitch Mirka's got more self-control than you when she's in heat. Either you come back home or I'll drag you back, do you hear?"

If there had been a well in the garden, I'd have thrown myself down it to hide myself from the Roolands' horrified stares, not to mention those of the neighbours who'd been brought out onto their doorsteps by Arthur's ranting.

"Listen to me, Arthur," I said through gritted teeth, and grabbed him by the wrist. The look in my eyes must have told him I meant business. He shut up.

"If you carry on like this, I'll go and get Mum. We'll be out of this town before you know it, both of us, and then you'll be all alone in your poxy little house. Understand? Do you understand, Arthur?"

That certainly sobered him up a bit. He turned on his heels and made himself scarce. I ran back into the house like a madwoman, tore up the stairs to my bedroom on all fours, threw myself on my bed and burst into floods of tears. After a few moments, I recognized Monsieur Rooland's footsteps on the staircase. "He's come to give me the sack," I thought. Who could blame him? He couldn't have Arthur singing serenades like that outside his house. It was over.

He came into my room.

"Hello, Louise."

Seen through my tears, he was more handsome than ever. He was smiling.

"It's nothing. Please don't cry."

"Are you angry with me?"

"Why would I be angry? It's not your fault!"

I fell back onto the bed, burying my face in the pillow. "Thank you!" I sobbed.

I'm not sure if he heard me, but he stroked my hair, softly, before he left the room.

SEVEN

Life continued like that for a few months, and in the end I think I managed to find myself a sort of quiet happiness. It wasn't the happiness I'd expected—it wasn't so glamorous, or so much fun—but the more I think about it, the more it seems to me that it *was* a real happiness all the same. One thing surprised me to begin with—the way Madame Rooland got when she was drunk. Normally when people have had a few they get all talkative, excited; they wave their arms about, shout or laugh. Thelma was silent, though, like she was thinking deep, private thoughts. It was only come the evening, in the living room, that she livened up a bit to put on her show for Jess... or during the night when the booze stopped her from sleeping and she got up to play records. When winter came, there was a slight change in the after-dinner routine. Instead of putting on her dressing gown, Madame Rooland would put on a fur coat. She had a beautiful one, made of long, soft, light-brown fur. I don't know what creature they had to skin for it. Maybe mink? Fur coats aren't my strong suit.

Anyway, the first time I saw her naked underneath that beautiful coat I didn't like it at all.

I mean, you're meant to wear a dressing gown next to the skin, right? A coat, though, with nothing underneath—if you ask me, that looks strange... But when you're a maid, you shouldn't let anything surprise you. The boss is always right, or at least you've got to act like they are. All their odd habits and vices are perfectly respectable, because they pay you to respect them. Each to their own.

And so, winter came. They're never white, round here, even when it snows a lot—they're filthy and grey. Winters of mud and soot that make Léopoldville look like a sick old lady.

One evening, Monsieur Rooland came home with something on his mind. Since the cold had set in he'd started wearing an overcoat with epaulettes that made him look like some sort of army officer. He spent a long time talking to his wife, who by some miracle was less hammered than usual. Then they called me into the living room. I'd lit a log fire earlier—now the wood crackled in the fireplace, filling the room with a homely pine-resin smell.

"Louise, I wanted to let you know that we're going to be hosting a party here on Sunday evening."

"Very good, Monsieur."

That gave me a twinge of anxiety in my gut somehow. It wasn't the thought of all the extra work that scared me—more the idea of our quiet home life being disturbed.

"There will be fifteen guests…"

This time it really was the thought of the work that gave me a fright. How was I going to feed and serve so many people?

"Fifteen to dinner, Monsieur!"

He shook his head.

"Oh, no, Louise! Not a dinner *à la française*—a buffet. You prepare lots of cold things and lay them out on a big table, you see? Club sandwiches, little snacks and so on."

I breathed a sigh of relief.

"OK!"

I'd started saying "OK", but I didn't have the right nasal pronunciation and it always got a little laugh out of Thelma and Jess.

"My bosses will be there, and my colleagues too: British, Belgians, Americans, some French… I really want everything to go well. Would you feel up to organizing it all?"

"Yes, Monsieur."

"I've always used the Hôtel Benoît until now—they prepare everything and send me someone to help with serving. But my wife and I think you're such a marvellous cook…"

"I'll handle it all myself, Monsieur. Madame will only have to explain to me—"

"That's just what I wanted to hear, Louise!" he cried. "I'll be there too, and I'll give you a hand."

And with that, what had felt like a sentence of forced labour suddenly seemed like a picnic to me. And it was too, or at least the preparations were.

You know, when you've got fire in your belly you can work wonders. I'm not quite saying what I did that Sunday was a miracle, but I'd like to see another maid do better.

On the Saturday afternoon, we went to Paris together to get our supplies, all three of us. I was in the back of the car, imagining I was a rich heiress being driven to a party by her chauffeur. Jess left the car in the American car park on the Rue Marbeuf, and we took a taxi to the *grands magasins*. Before we could think about the feast, we needed something to serve it on—I bought a stack of gold-coloured cardboard plates, and piles of paper lace serviettes. It was a funny feeling—the Roolands obeying my every word and gesture, as if they were my skivvies rather than my bosses. Since it was only a couple of weeks till Christmas I suggested we get some sparkly decorations to hang about the house. I also told them a candlelit soirée would be more atmospheric, so they bought a load of candles of all different colours and sizes, and some plastic candelabras into the bargain.

After all that, we went to the market at Les Halles—I needed chickens, a cut of beef, cheeses, prawns and fruit. We chose the best they had, and let me tell you something for free: money is beautiful. At home, on the rare occasions we ate chicken, Mum would always choose the cheapest one. There was more bone than meat, the flesh was colourless and the lumpy skin was covered in stubble. The ones we took home that day, though, they were another story: plump and delicious, looking good enough to eat raw, each one with a "Poulet de Bresse" medal round its neck.

When we got home, I stayed in charge. It was a lot for me to take on. Four chickens and a great big fillet of beef to cook—it was a mountain to climb, but I managed it. Then, with pans gently bubbling away on all hobs of the cooker, I got on the telephone and ordered an industrial quantity of rolls from the local baker. It was such a thrill for me, running the whole operation like that. Next to me, on the kitchen table, Jess was trimming the candles to fit them in the candelabras. His wife helped him for a while, then she disappeared, and soon we heard "Loving You" playing upstairs. Casually, Jess went to take a look in the living room. The bottle of Scotch was gone.

We gave each other a silent look. He went back to trimming his candles.

*

By Sunday evening, everything was ready. It was like a fairy-land! A few years earlier I'd seen a wonderful nativity scene in a big Paris church whose name I can't remember—Saint something-or-other. Anyway, even that wasn't as beautiful as the Roolands' dining room that evening.

We'd pushed the dinner table up against the far wall, along with another table so that we could fit everything on. On the smaller of the two, I'd arranged all the glasses: champagne flutes and big tumblers for the whisky. Resting in a gigantic washing basin that Mr Rooland had wrapped in holly branches were two bottles of Pommery champagne, covered in a pile of crushed ice, only their little golden caps poking out of the top. Such a pretty picture!

The bottles of whisky were lined up on the tabletop. All the big brands were there—Jess could get all the booze he needed at a good price from NATO headquarters.

The big table was for the buffet proper. If you could only see my chickens sitting on their golden plates, with their beds of cress and sliced tomatoes! I would have liked to have pho-tographs taken of them, in colour. And my sandwiches! With beef, anchovies, prawns, cheese—mountains of them. Fifteen people would never eat all that! We'd have leftovers for a week.

When the decorations were up, the candles lit, the cakes all laid out and adorned with little festive figures, Monsieur Rooland put his hands on my shoulders.

"This is magnificent, Louise. Congratulations."

He'd put on a midnight-blue suit with a white shirt and a beige tie. His hair smelt wonderful.

Madame Rooland was wearing a lamé sheath dress that clung to her like a second skin. You could see what good shape she was in. Her breasts were high and firm, her waist no bigger than a napkin ring, and her hips swelled out gently below, like the body of one of those opaline vases you see in antique-shop windows. She'd made herself up more heavily than usual too. Her lipstick was mauve rather than orange and her foundation made her cheekbones stand out.

"How beautiful Madame is!" I cried.

Jess seemed happy at that. He took Thelma by the waist and pulled her powerfully up against him, which she told him off for, saying he was going to crease her dress! Just then, the doorbell rang. The first guests had arrived.

There was an American general, in civilian dress. He was still young but had snow-white hair, which gave him quite a distinguished air. His wife and daughter were with him. Next, a French couple arrived. They spoke American just as well as Jess, but they seemed awkward and didn't know what to do with their hands. And then the Léopoldville police commissioner turned up—just a big kid, really, gloomy and nervous. I think Jess had taken pity on him. Sometimes he'd hang about in front of the house like I used to do.

After him, the other guests arrived all at once, and I was overwhelmed. Suddenly it was like a busy railway station in there—all the chatter, the laughter… And boozing—you'd have to see it to believe it! At our dinner parties in France we chat a bit first, then we drink a bit and get a little more lively, but it's only by dessert that people are merry enough to start singing or telling dirty jokes. With the Americans, it's totally different. Everyone grabs a glass and a bottle of whisky and sets about getting drunk like it's going out of style.

Within half an hour, apart from the young commissioner, they were all sloshed, including the French couple, who'd been at the champagne. The husband had overcome his shyness and was clowning about, with the metal cap from a cork screwed into his eye like a monocle.

Suddenly, Jess clapped his hands and they all stampeded towards the buffet. The general's daughter was an ugly little thing in glasses, and hadn't been to finishing school yet if the way she tore at her chicken leg was anything to go by. I hope for her sake there isn't any cold chicken on the menu the first time a boy asks her out to dinner. Meanwhile I stood by attentively, offering round condiments for the food and ice for the whiskies.

A few of the men tried flirting with me a bit, but I couldn't understand their lines, so it didn't go anywhere and I was able to get away with a polite smile.

When they'd eaten their fill, they started drinking again, and now things started getting *really* ugly. I had to take the French lady to the toilet to be sick. Thelma started up the record player, playing jazz, slow dances and rock 'n' roll. I couldn't move any more for all the people dancing. (Those who were still standing, that is—some of them were already snoozing in the living-room armchairs.)

Thelma was more out of it than any of them, jumping up and down, clapping her hands in front of the commissioner, who didn't know what to do with himself. At one point, she tripped and fell onto the carpet. The commissioner went to help her up, but as he bent over the general shoved him in the side and he ended up on top of her. They all howled with laughter. I tried to catch Jess's eye. He seemed to find it funny too. Strange people: if you tried a stunt like that at one of our local dances it would cause a riot.

To make matters worse, Thelma didn't even try to get up, just writhed around on the floor in front of everyone, striking all sorts of poses. I felt so embarrassed for Monsieur Rooland, and for the young commissioner, who was trying unsuccessfully to get away from her.

Jess must not have cared, or else he had a bloody strong character to put up with nonsense like that!

EIGHT

It was turning into an absolute nightmare; at least it was for me, tired and worn out as I was after two days of preparations. If I hadn't found their antics so awful, I might even have had a couple of glasses of champagne myself, just so I could know what it's like to be in that happy state where even the worst behaviour apparently seems completely normal.

Fifteen was actually the right number for that sort of party—it allowed for a kind of rotation system, with those waking up from their drunken snoozes replacing those who were just passing out. My parquet was like a pigsty floor. It was going to take a lot of scrubbing, sweat and steel wool to get it looking respectable again. Through all the confusion, I kept watching Monsieur Rooland. Seeing everyone cutting loose, he'd decided to do the same and was dancing a cha-cha-cha with the general's wife, who was taller than him, a proper skyscraper. As I was carrying out a tray of dirty glasses, one of the guests grabbed me by the waist and pulled me towards him to dance—a stocky bloke with a crew cut, and fishy eyes behind his gold-rimmed glasses.

I tried to put up a fight—it's not the maid's place to be dancing with the guests—but he wouldn't take no for an answer. My tray fell to the floor and everyone burst out laughing. The American was holding me so tightly to his chest that I was short of breath. So I danced with him, not that I had any choice in the matter. He deliberately trampled on the broken glasses as we swayed. When the record finished, we were near the door to the corridor. He dragged me through it. As it was supposed to be a candlelit soirée, Monsieur Rooland had cut the electricity, just in case anyone was tempted to flick a light switch. That meant some areas of the house were in darkness, including the hallway, which was practically pitch black. My gallant shoved me roughly up against the wall and tried to kiss me. I struggled as much as I could, but the bloke was as strong as an ox. When he found he couldn't kiss me on the mouth, he started hitching up my dress. That was more than I could stand, and I screamed for Monsieur Rooland at the top of my voice.

Jess arrived quicker than I could have hoped. He took his guest by the arm and told him off in a friendly tone, while my attacker bent down and pretended to tie his shoelace, hiding his embarrassment.

We'd both let our guards down, Monsieur Rooland and me, when his guest suddenly grabbed the bottom of my dress and pulled it right up in a flash, all the way up to my waist, like skinning a rabbit! It was quite a tight dress—the one from the funeral, if you remember?—and it took me a moment to pull it back down over my bare legs, as I'd filled out since I bought it, especially round the hips... When I eventually managed to get it readjusted, I looked up to see my chubby dance partner laid out on the corridor floor, Monsieur Rooland having just clocked him one on the jaw. Good old Jess was kneeling down next to him now, shaking his head and repeating in English, "Sorry, Dick! Sorry!"

I was sorrier than anyone. I'd put so much effort, so much thought into that party, and to see it turn out like it did... I felt rotten, as I'm sure you can imagine.

At my wits' end, I went outside. The night air smelt of sadness. It was freezing cold, like all the winter evenings round here. A white fog filled the road. The guests' cars were all lined up bumper-to-bumper on the drive, glistening weirdly like animals gleaming with sweat. I went and looked at them to give myself something else to think about. Their roofs and windows were all covered in rime, but it was the insides of the cars that I was most interested in, so I scraped some of the frost off with my fingernails to see through. I was only wearing my old black dress, but I didn't feel cold. I went from car to car, forcing myself to admire them, to distract myself from the fury burning inside me, making me tremble with rage.

And that's when I saw two figures hunched in the third car. I felt a rush of fear—a couple of thieves must have been going through the vehicles and hidden themselves when they saw me approaching. I turned and fled back to the house as fast as I could. My dance companion was back on his feet, slapping Monsieur Rooland heartily on the back. Apparently he found being punched in the face the height of hilarity. Jess was laughing too—everything for the best in the best of all possible worlds.

"Monsieur, come quickly, I think they're stealing things from the cars."

He followed me. Once we were outside, I whispered:

"They're hiding over there, in the third car along."

He counted with his finger—one, two, three…

"That one?"

"Yes."

He sprang towards the vehicle. It struck me how rashly he was acting. If the thieves were armed he could get shot!

"Don't, Jess! I'll get the commissioner."

And I shouted:

"Commissioner, help, they're robbing the cars!"

Jess didn't seem to hear me, so I rushed after him, to hold him back, but his hand was already on the door handle. When you open the door on one of these cars, the light comes on automatically inside. A white glare lit up the interior. Jess froze, and so did I when I saw it: there were no thieves, just Madame Rooland and the white-haired general. I'll never dare say what they were doing in there. For as long as I live I'll remember those two bleary faces turning towards us, blinking like a couple of owls woken at midday. Their eyes were all bloodshot, and their skin was so red it looked as if their heads had been boiled. The commissioner had come running too, and took it all in with sad sigh.

Monsieur Rooland slammed the door shut again, and the whole scene was lost in darkness. Then Jess did something I didn't see coming: he slapped me. I don't know if he thought I'd deliberately lured him out there, or if he was just taking out his anger on me… As he slapped me, he shouted something in his language. I didn't understand, but I knew it was an insult from the look that went along with it. And that was when the sorrow hit me: an immense, total sorrow, like I didn't believe it was possible for a human being to feel. I broke down in tears next to the car, while the two shadows continued to move behind the frosted windows.

Jess had gone back inside. I looked up at the sky. I wanted it to see my unhappiness. But there were no fluffy clouds and tropical seas up there any more, just our poisonous Léopoldville sky.

An unfriendly sky. One that said "no" to the people down below. I went stiffly over to the gate, like a robot. The dead, empty, echoing street swallowed me up.

I walked back home in a daze, just like the old days.

NINE

It must have been at least two in the morning when I came to a stop in front of Arthur's place. He and Mum would have hit the sack hours ago. I hesitated. My cheek was still burning from the slap. My heart too. I took a handful of gravel and threw it against their bedroom-window shutters. Mum's always been a shallow sleeper. A light went on in the room straight away, spilling out through the gaps in the wooden slats. Then a window opened, and I recognized her little wedge-shaped face, her scruffy hair falling down over her eyes.

"It's me, Mum!"

"God, what time do you call this?"

That brought me back down to earth. If I told her everything she'd never let me go back to the Roolands', and I was already starting to miss my island.

She didn't have a dressing gown, my mum, just one of her dad's old postman's capes that she'd put on when she got up at night. While she was sorting herself out, I heard Arthur's grumpy voice asking her what was going on. In the dead silence of the night there was something terribly embarrassing about the rudely awoken couple's squabbling being broadcast to the world.

At last, she opened the door. I'd hardly set foot inside before she exclaimed:

"What's going on? You been crying?"

"I'll explain tomorrow."

"Oh, will you now? No, Missy, you'll tell me right away!"

Whenever she said "Missy" you knew things were hotting up. I hadn't heard her call me that since the day she caught me bunking off school. She was a funny sight in her nightdress and old postie's cape, like something from a comic strip.

"Come on, I'm waiting!"

We could hear that idiot Arthur upstairs, putting his trousers on and looking for his slippers under the bed.

"Spit it out, quick, before Arthur comes down."

"There was a party… One of the guests was a bit drunk. He took me aside and tried to feel me up, so I gave him a slap."

"Good for you," she said. "And then what?"

"Well, I felt bad. Ashamed. You know how it is, don't you? So I left."

"Just like that?"

"Yes, just like that! You don't stop to think in those situations."

Mum glared at me. She wasn't buying it. She could smell something fishy in my story, and I could tell she wanted to grill me some more, but we could hear Arthur's clumsy step coming down the rickety wooden staircase, so she didn't dare.

Even when he's dressed up to the nines Arthur's not much to look at, but woken in the middle of the night he's downright terrifying. He had on a mouldy old vest, which he wore constantly because he used to have trouble with his lungs. Unshaven, puffy eyed, his toes sticking through the holes in his slippers, he looked like someone you'd see in a photo in a true-crime magazine—Psycho of the Month!

It'd been weeks since I'd set foot at home. Seeing them both still looking the same, so scruffy and scrawny—it made me choke. I regretted it now—running off into the night like that. No, Arthur's place would never be any kind of refuge for me.

"What is it now?"

That was very like him, that "now". As if I made a habit of dragging them out of bed at two in the morning!

I couldn't bring myself to explain, so Mum did it for me.

"They've got people round at the Yanks' place."

At the Yanks' place! Who gave her the right to call them that? And where did that snobby tone come from? Her with her hare-lip, she was hardly the classiest lady in town. What reason did she have to look down on the Roolands? People will never get on as long as there's prejudice in the world, I thought to myself.

"…they're all sloshed round there, and one of them tried it on with Louise so she gave him a smack."

Arthur's eyes twinkled with a cruel satisfaction.

"And, of course, now they've shown her the door?"

"No, she did a runner!"

He was a bit disappointed at that, but he soon found a way back onto his high horse.

"I knew this would happen."

"Why do you say that?" I protested.

"I remember that Sunday when you were acting the tart with them in the garden… Didn't I warn you, back when all this started? They're nothing but a pack of animals, those American blokes."

I could have scratched his eyes out.

"I'll go and give 'em a piece of my mind tomorrow, the dirty buggers."

"It's not their fault! One of their guests was drunk—so what? It could've happened to anyone!"

"Listen to you sticking up for them now!" roared Arthur. "If you're so fond of them, why have you come running back here in the middle of the night?"

"Fine! If that's how it is I'll go back."

I was already at the door. Mum caught hold of my arm.

"Got to your room."

"But—"

"Now!"

I felt like I was ten years old again. I did as I was told.

I didn't have a big bedroom, but it was so sparsely furnished, with just an iron bed, a chair and a coat stand, that it seemed huge. I was in tears as I got undressed. The room smelt of damp, and mouldy wallpaper. The sheets were cold, and every time I moved the springs would twang, sending vibrations through the whole bed. I just wanted to get to sleep. Right then, the idea of unconsciousness seemed like paradise to me. I wanted to forget Jess Rooland and his eyes so full of hurt, boring into me. I wanted to forget Thelma's dazed features blinking up at us as the car light went on and we saw her there, half naked underneath the general... Other faces filled the darkness too, dancing a terrifying waltz around me. My chubby dance partner with his fishy eyes, the French guest playing the fool with the cork cap screwed into his eye. As we danced I heard the miserable sound of broken glasses crunching under our feet, and the screaming of the black singers' voices coming from the record player. Everything looked different in the flickering candlelight. When I finally fell asleep I dreamt that all the guests were lying dead, their waxy faces lit up by altar candles.

*

"Louiiiiise!"

It was Mum's voice, ridiculously shrill when she shouted.

I was wide awake instantly. My worries of the night before were all still there. The dull light of a gloomy day filled the room. From the bedroom window I could see the chimneys of the chemical plant, already spewing brown smoke into the air.

"Louiiiiiise!"

"Yes! What is it?"

"Come down here."

What time was it? I could sense the day was already well under way. I'm not sure how I could tell. Just something in the air, I suppose—lots of tiny little clues.

I put on my black dress again, since it was the only one I had with me. The comforting smell of coffee wafted up from the kitchen.

That was always the one good thing at our place—the coffee. Mum's crazy about it. She puts her heart and soul into making it like only a real coffee lover can. We don't always have meat for the pot, it's true, but our coffee's always top quality.

I pushed open the door. The first thing I saw, because I was looking for it, was the big kitchen clock on the sideboard. Ten o'clock. That meant Arthur would be at work, which perked me up no end.

"Morning, Mum!"

She smiled stiffly back at me, and it was only then that I looked around and noticed Madame Rooland. She was sitting at the table, in front of a steaming cup of coffee, all fresh-faced and smiling.

"Hello, Louise!"

Just like that, I swear: "Hello, Louise!" She knew I'd caught her messing around with the general last night, but here she was, bright and cheery, as if nothing had happened. Shameless, she was.

"Good morning, Madame."

"Not too tired today?"

"No, Madame."

She'd come to take me back. I was pleased, but I wondered what she'd told Mum. I hadn't thought of that when I'd invented my lie the previous night. Things couldn't have gone too badly if Mum had made her coffee, though.

I stood there like a lemon, like in my oral at school when the examiner asked me to list all the different fossil fuels. I knew what I should say but I didn't dare. The situation was all wrong. Mum and Madame Rooland were never supposed to meet each other. Thelma in Arthur's kitchen, in front of a cup of coffee—like on the day of that exam, it just didn't seem real.

Back then, I told myself the examiner probably couldn't care less about fossil fuels. Maybe he cared even less than I did. And what did I need to know about all that to go and work at Ridel's anyway? It was just a game, like one of those quizzes you see on the telly.

"You want some coffee, Louise?"

"Yes, Mum."

"Madame Rooland" (she pronounced it "Rolon") "has come to take you back. She was very surprised to find that you'd gone. I told her I don't like these goings-on very much. Even in high society" (a note of bitterness crept into her voice on those words) "a guest can't allow himself to go taking liberties with a young girl. I've always brought you up well; you've had an education and everything…"

The proud, virtuous mother, showing this rich foreigner that her daughter wasn't just anybody.

While she gave her speech, Thelma was staring at the calendar hanging on the wall. She seemed fascinated. It showed a little girl with blonde plaits riding a pony, I remember. She didn't give a damn about Mum's sermon. She'd come to get me because she needed me. I was just a useful household appliance that allowed her to live as she pleased.

Mum turned towards her.

"I'm wondering if it's wise to let her go back to you, Madame Rooland. At seventeen, a young girl…"

Jess must have told her she had free rein. Thelma took two ten-thousand-franc notes from her pocket, folded them in four, and placed them on the tabletop, next to a sugar bowl with Bonaparte's thin face on it. He glared sternly at Mum.

"What's that?" she asked softly, a note of fear in her voice.

"My husband he is telling me that it is to compensate Louise of the good work she did at the weekend."

Poor Mum's mouth was hanging open. I don't know if twenty thousand francs seems like a lot to you, but it's always been a fortune in our house. There are people who couldn't make it go very far, but Mum can work miracles with bit of extra cash. You should see her when her book of coupons is full and she goes to swap it for five hundred francs' worth of stuff from the grocer—you wouldn't believe how much she comes back with!

"If my girl's happy to go back, Madame, I can't go against her wishes. We don't like making a fuss round here."

TEN

She didn't have the car, so we walked back to the island.

I was surprised to see that she and her husband had cleared all the mess away. I only had to do the dishes and scrub the floor. You could still smell the piss-up, though—the living room stank of stale cigars, spilt champagne… and vomit, I'm afraid to say. Thelma stayed off the sauce that day, helping me with the housework like a good girl. She contented herself with chain-smoking Camels while she dried the dishes.

At one point—in the afternoon, I think—she asked me:

"Why did you leave?"

I looked her in the face.

"It was seeing you in the car with that white-haired bloke. It was disgusting."

"What is it mean, 'disgusting'?"

"It… it upset me. It was shameful."

"Oh, yes?"

"Yes. Especially in front of your husband."

"Jess saw?"

"Yes!"

It didn't seem to bother her in the slightest. I still can't believe he hadn't told her. What a world!

And to take the biscuit, behind the cloud of blue smoke from her cigarette, she was smiling. A little half-smile, just one eye and the corner of her mouth.

"He must feel terrible about it, don't you think?"

"Jess? Oh, no!"

"But he loves you!"

"Certainly, very much."

"So…"

I had a dish in my hands, but I felt too weak to dry it.

"You are little girl, you are not to understand."

"Well, then I wonder who *could* understand all this?"

She sat down at the table, pushing aside some crockery to make room for her elbows.

"Jess wanted a child. We had one who is not come to his birth, you see? Since then, I cannot have one any more, and our… conjugal life—is that what you say?"

"Yes, if you like!"

"Our conjugal life is like a walk in the woods in winter. There are no leaves, no flowers, just the black branches."

I had tears in my eyes. I put down my plate and went to put my arms around her. We all have our sorrows, you see, even Americans.

Everything started up again, just like before. We never mentioned that horrible evening again. The only change was that, from then on, they started to go out more in the evenings. They'd go to Paris or to see a show. It was as if they were scared to spend their evenings at home together like they had before. To begin with I'd go to bed as soon as they left, but I couldn't sleep all alone in that big house, so I started waiting up for them with a book.

It wasn't a bad way to spend the evening at all. I'd sit on the sofa, in front of the fireplace, a log fire crackling in the hearth. Now and then I'd break off from my reading and prick up my

moaning in the chimney. The fire was burning high. I went back to my book. It was a romance, which would normally have had me gripped, but I couldn't follow the twists and turns of the plot. I was waiting—do you understand? Waiting for a vague something that, deep down, I knew was coming. And then it came—the harsh trill of the telephone. We barely used it at all at the Roolands'—just for placing orders with shopkeepers. I'd certainly never heard it ringing in the middle of the night. I looked at the time—twenty past midnight. I got that from Mum, that glance at the clock. We were always wary of anything out of the ordinary at home. I hesitated. There was a bleakness to the telephone's ring. Eventually I answered it. I heard a man's voice, a stranger's, choked with emotion:

"Come to the station, right away. Something's happened. It's a bad business."

That was all he said. Not a word more. He didn't even make sure that I'd heard him, just hung up the receiver. A bad business! My legs were trembling, a feeling of emptiness filled my chest and a chill ran through my teeth. Yes—my teeth. Odd, isn't it? I thought about the noise I'd heard earlier—I felt sure that was the "bad business".

I set off at a run, splashing down flooded streets, stumbling, gasping, the rain drenching me, running into my nose and mouth—and at every step I was crying out inside: "Jess! Oh, Jess! Don't let it be true. Jess, my love."

Arriving at the level crossing, I saw that it was more than a bad business: it was a disaster. The embankment was crowded with people. A train sat on the tracks, in a place where you'd never see one stopped usually. Its engine coughed great clouds of smoke and flashes of flame into the dark, rainy night.

Mum had told me about the war. About how she'd been caught up in a bombing raid. Her stories had conjured up all sorts of images like the scene in front of me now.

I pushed my way into the murmuring crowd. People moved aside to let me through. I didn't have too much trouble getting to where it was—to where Monsieur Rooland's beautiful green car, or at least what remained of it after it had been crushed and folded in two, was lying on its side. The bodywork wasn't gleaming any more; it was crumpled up like a ball of paper. The rails and the embankment were strewn with metal debris: I recognized one of the bumpers, Madame Rooland's beautiful crocodile-skin handbag, the windscreen, some scraps of white leather… The station staff were swarming round the wreck. I joined them. A big bloke, whose face I knew, asked me what I was playing at.

"It's Monsieur and Madame Rooland…"

He was dripping wet, water streaming down either side of his black visor. A flicker of understanding showed on his ruddy, mustachioed face.

"Oh! You're the girl the man was talking about."

"What man?"

"The one who was in there! The driver, I mean."

Since the telephone call my thoughts had all been in a muddle. I'd been swept up by some sort of awful merry-go-round, spinning in the pouring rain. Suddenly, hearing those words, I felt a surprising calm come over me.

"He isn't dead?"

It was as if Jess was there in front of me: his polite, slightly sad smile, his freckles, his gentle eyes. I'd thought him swallowed up for ever by some kind of endless nothingness. That was the "bad business" for me. If he was still alive then there *was* no bad business.

"He is, the lucky devil. Are you a relative?"

"His maid."

The other rescuers paid us no attention. They were puffing and gasping, straining to tip the car off its side so they could open one of the doors. I saw then that there was still someone inside… I recognized Thelma's mauve dress and her white fur stole. The red-faced railwayman stared at me grimly.

He was holding a lantern in his hand, one of the two-coloured ones they have for signalling, lighting up the wreck for his mates while he talked. I'd only just noticed that detail. The world was coming into focus, but agonizingly slowly, like a jigsaw I was putting together bit by bit.

"How did it happen?"

"We don't know much yet… The level-crossing barrier must have been up. What with all the rain, he must have missed the train pulling out of the station. It ran right into them. Luckily for him the door on his side flew open with the impact. He was thrown out."

"Is he hurt?"

"I don't think it's too bad."

"Where is he?"

"They took him to hospital. He didn't want to go, with his wife still in there… But they made him, so he asked us to let you know."

I heard sobbing close by, in the darkness. A flash of red light from the lantern lit up La Magnin, the fat barrier operator, standing in the middle of a group of silent spectators.

She had her dressing gown on, bare legs underneath; the rain had plastered her hair to her sickly-looking face. She was crying and moaning, shaking her head as if not wanting to accept what had happened.

The other watchers were standing stock-still, looking on in solemn silence, oblivious to the raging storm, shocked and unsettled at the sight of the mangled car.

"Is she dead?"

"Probably. We'll see soon…"

I didn't say anything else, just stayed next to the man with the lantern. It was an awfully sinister scene. Every now and then a shaft of light from the lamp, or a flash of flame from the locomotive farther up the track, would light up the wreck, and for a second I'd see Madame Rooland squashed up inside the mass of crumpled metal.

I thought of her sprawled on the sofa, in her orange shorts and green blouse, listening to "Loving You" and drinking a glass of whisky. I thought of that time in the kitchen, her drying the plates while she told me that her marriage was like a walk in the woods in winter… Was it really over, all that? Did none of that mean anything any more? Had Time really snatched back all those moments, those words, those scenes? What would Jess's life be like now?

"Onetwothree, *heave*! Onetwothree, *heave*!" they chanted, like a gang of workmen. A couple of days earlier they'd replaced the wooden signpost on our road with a concrete one, and to keep in time the workers had repeated the same cry, over and over.

They rolled the car back onto what was left of its wheels.

A big bloke started whacking away at something with a hammer.

"Easy there!"

"Get her legs free first."

They were talking in hushed voices, but every now and then I could hear the odd word, forced out at a higher pitch by the effort they were making.

"Whoa, whoa, go easy there now! She's still breathing…"

So that's all it is, I said to myself. It's just a crumpled-up car with Madame Rooland inside. They'll get her out… Soon the trains will be running like normal again. Tomorrow Jess will buy another car. The next day maybe Thelma will be back on her feet, with the help of some crutches. Soon there'll just be a bit of broken glass here at the side of the railway line to remind us of…

Life goes on regardless—I knew that was true now. The earth's wounds always heal. There's no sickness the world can't survive.

They were moving away from the car now, like a funny little swarm of ants. I saw that they'd managed to get Thelma out. They didn't lay her down on the ground, just kept on carrying her down the embankment, the bloke with the lantern lighting the way.

The ambulance was waiting on the road running alongside the railway tracks.

It was the lantern man again who gave me a hand climbing up into the back.

"She's the maid. The husband wanted her to go along with his wife," he explained to the others.

And then I was inside—an iron cage lit by the harsh light of a bare bulb. The doors closed behind me. I was alone in the back with Thelma, sitting next to the stretcher on a little fold-down leather seat. I hadn't got a proper look at her until then.

It was mostly her legs that were hurt. Below her ankles they were just a mangled mess. Her arms were badly cut up too. Ghastly streams of blood ran in rivulets over the rubber of the stretcher. She had a purple bruise the size of a fist over her right eye and an open wound on the top of her head, staining her hair a strange colour.

Her face was pale, her nose wrinkled up. Her breathing seemed ragged and shallow. The ambulance must have been going flat out. We were taking the corners at speed, jolting me from one side to the other, with nothing but the cloth curtain separating me from the driver to hang on to. At one point I lost my balance and fell onto the stretcher. That was when she opened her eyes. They weren't the dazed eyes of someone coming to and struggling to understand where they are and what has happened to them. Not a bit of it—her eyes were clear. She understood.

"It's me, Madame…"

Thelma looked at me like she had that first day, when I went to offer my services to them. Oh God, what was she thinking? It felt like she wanted to tell me something important.

"Are you in pain?"

I was leaning over the stretcher. I put my body between her and the light, so her face stayed in the shadows. I didn't have the guts to look into those piercing eyes. I felt like she could see right to the heart of me, like she could see that great truth I hadn't even been aware of myself until an hour before.

A walk in the woods in winter, she'd said…

"Are you in pain?"

I couldn't think of anything else to say. But I didn't just say it, I shouted it at the top of my lungs. I couldn't help myself. I had to do something to break the evil spell she was casting.

"Are you in pain?"

She didn't have the strength to keep her eyes open. They closed slowly, like flowers going to sleep with the setting of the sun. I stayed in the same position for a moment more, then a bend in the road threw me back to the other side of the ambulance. I sat back on the seat, but facing towards the doors this time—I didn't dare look at her any more.

ELEVEN

I'd been to the hospital once before, when Arthur had his fistula, and I had awful memories of it. The one in our town's like a prison—a horrid grey place with bars on the windows and a wall running around it that's far too high for just a hospital. The second they opened the doors of the ambulance I threw myself outside. The breakneck ride had destroyed my nerves. The storm had blown itself out. There were still a few gusts of wind and rain, but the sky was clearing already and from time to time the moon showed itself through a rent in the clouds.

Some male nurses slid the stretcher out of the ambulance. I stood back to give them room and watched the sad procession disappear into the building. I didn't dare follow. I was terrified of the place. The ambulance driver took pity on me.

"Oi, darling, don't stay there. Get inside, you're shivering."

He was right. Long shudders were shaking my shoulders and my teeth were chattering. I went up the concrete ramp to the entrance. The only light in the foyer came from two blue-tinted light bulbs. The walls were painted a muddy green. A withered plant sat in a gigantic flowerpot, probably a donation from some grateful patient. Wooden benches ran the length of the room, from one door to the other. I sat down to wait, and tried to get my thoughts in order, but I was on the merry-go-round again! A mad, muddled merry-go-round but, instead of wooden horses, all the actors in the drama of my life were there, fixed in terrifying poses: Mum with her purple harelip and Granddad's old postman's cape; Arthur in front of the telly, cheering on a wrestler; Madame Rooland, drunk on her sofa; and finally, Monsieur Rooland, holding a steering wheel—one without a car attached. In the background others were spinning: the white-haired general, the railway worker with the lantern… Not people I cared about particularly, but they had their place in my memories regardless.

I must have been sitting there for quite a while. The hospital seemed deserted. Now and then a woman's screams would ring out, but the second they stopped, a dead silence would fall in the building.

Suddenly an old nun appeared from a corridor, the wings of her gigantic wimple beating the air like those of some great seabird trying to take flight. She wore iron-rimmed glasses and was clutching a ball of blue wool to her starched white dress. She seemed surprised to see me.

"Are you waiting for someone, my child?"

I wasn't waiting for some*one*, I was waiting for some*thing*: an answer from Fate.

"I'm a maid. I work for the couple they just brought in, Sister."

She nodded.

"Were you in the car?"

"No, Sister."

A silence. Again the invisible woman's scream tore through the hospital's suffocating calm. Without thinking, I asked:

"Why is she screaming?"

"She's in labour."

I blushed, stupidly, to hear a nun use that word. But despite her clothes this old lady didn't seem like a bride of Christ, really—more like one of those old nurses who bicycle all over the countryside giving injections. Everything about her gave off an air of firmness, goodness, activity. She must have a lot of authority in the hospital and know how to talk to the patients, I thought.

"Do you have any news on my employers, Sister?"

"The gentleman isn't very seriously hurt. Just a gash on his shin and a dislocated shoulder…"

She stopped and looked at me, asking herself if I could take what was to follow.

"His wife is dead?"

"Yes."

The merry-go-round came to a halt, like a spinning roulette wheel. There was no more Thelma. Her winter walk in the woods was over.

I looked away and my eyes came to rest on the jagged-edged leaves of the pot plant. A philodendron! I'd always remembered that strange name. The leaves lower down were yellowing. The plant was going to die, just like Thelma Rooland. The air in the hospital didn't suit it at all—it was a delicate plant, it needed to be fussed over…

"Does he know?"

"Not yet."

"Can I see him?"

"Come with me."

She led the way, up a wooden staircase carpeted in spongy rubber. I seemed to interest her. She examined me over the tops of her glasses as we walked.

"Have you been with them for a long time?"

"A few months… Eight, I think."

"Are they foreign?"

We were still talking of "them" in the present tense. Thelma hadn't been consigned to the past yet, probably because her body was still warm, and lying not far away—a human presence. Tomorrow, or the day after, we'd give her over to the earth, and to the past tense.

"They're Americans, Sister."

"A tragic accident."

"Yes, Sister."

Jess was in a room on the first floor with one other patient: an old man, tall, thin and yellow with a white moustache. He was wide awake and watching Jess in silence. They'd put Mercurochrome on the grazes on Jess's face, and it made him look quite different. His head was buried in a gigantic pillow, and it looked so fragile to me there, like a child's.

"Hello, Louise."

He still had the voice of a man—of a tough man, ashamed of his weaknesses and trying to stay in control.

"Oh, Monsieur!"

I'd stopped, unable to go any closer. Seeing him alive and well in that strange bed had brought on a wave of giddiness, like vertigo.

"How is my wife? Do you have any news?"

The old nun went to his side, her clothes giving off a waft of ether as she moved. She sat down by the bed and took Jess's hand. He understood right away.

"Oh! I see," he stammered.

I wondered whether he would cry. But, no—he didn't break down, simply looked up at the ceiling. I was the one who burst into tears.

*

We stayed by his bedside for nearly an hour, without him speaking another word or even looking at us. From time to time his neighbour would cough—the only noise that disturbed the heavy silence in the room. It was as if we were hypnotized, the old nun and me—put in some agonizing trance by the sight of his silent suffering. What was going on behind the blank mask of Jess's face? What memories were haunting him? What thoughts were tormenting him? It seemed to us like he was on some long mental journey, reliving his life with Thelma, trying to understand how it could be that she was gone. A change was taking place right under our eyes, although we couldn't see it happening, and the consequences would be surprising.

We waited respectfully. Eventually Monsieur Rooland let out a long sigh, like a mathematician who'd just solved a complex equation.

"When can I get out of here?" he asked the nun.

"In two or three days, maybe sooner. We'll have to wait for the head doctor's decision. He'll see you tomorrow morning."

He gave a little nod of agreement.

"Louise…"

"Yes, Monsieur?"

"You'll be going back to your parents', I suppose?"

"No, Monsieur. If it's all right with you I'll stay at the house."

"All alone?"

I shivered. The island was a very different place now. I thought of the shutter banging against the wall, the wind howling in the chimney… and then, even worse, Thelma's bottles of Scotch, her glass, her terry-cloth dressing gown…

"Yes, Monsieur. All alone."

"And what will you do?"

"I'll get everything ready for when you come home."

That seemed to calm him. He nodded.

"Very well."

That was all. I wondered whether I should shake his hand, but he didn't hold it out for me, so I left, turning back for a last look when I reached the doorway. Jess was staring up at the ceiling again. I found myself following his gaze. It was a very dull, white ceiling with a glass globe light in the middle of it.

Had Jess Rooland ever imagined that one day he'd watch the film of his life projected onto such a lousy screen?

TWELVE

Apparently Arthur heard about it from the neighbours when he was setting off for work. He turned right around, went back to tell Mum and the clock hadn't struck eight before she arrived at the Roolands', done up to the nines, if you please. She'd even put on lipstick, which went some way towards hiding her harelip. I was still asleep—I hadn't got to bed till five. My head had hardly hit the pillow, with the covers pulled up over it, before I sank into a deep sleep.

"Louiiiiise!"

There was only one person in the world who called my name like that—like a peacock's squawk. I sat up in bed. I was groggy with tiredness, and my first thought was "Thelma's dead", but I didn't feel any regret. I was already thinking about her in the past tense. I pushed the shutters open. The night's storm had cleared the sky. The sun wasn't shining, though—it was too early for that. Round our way the sun has a lie-in every day, even the good days. Mum was down below, outside the door.

"I'm coming!"

The top-down perspective didn't do her any favours. She looked like some kind of disfigured dwarf, her upturned face ugly and coarse. Behind her, in the red sand of the driveway, you could still see the marks left by the green Dodge. The car was dead too. That beautiful, seductive car!

Everything would die, then. But Mum seemed very much alive. There was something grasping and greedy in her manner too. I'd never noticed that before—I mean, to me she was just Mum, right? She was how she was—the finished article. No point in judging her.

I went down to let her in, glancing nervously through the open door of the living room on the way, half expecting to see the memory of Thelma still lingering inside, but the room looked brand new. It had already forgotten the American woman. It was just a normal bourgeois living room again.

"Hello, Mum."

She came inside quickly, her eyes darting about to take everything in. She seemed strangely tense.

"I heard the news. Horrible. So, she's dead, your boss?"

"Yes."

"How did it happen?"

And, actually, I didn't know. No one had explained to me how the accident had come about. Of course I'd seen the train, and the mangled car on the embankment, but the details were a mystery to me. That left Mum, who'd been questioning me two seconds earlier, to fill *me* in. She'd bumped into some people on the way who were in the know. So, she'd only been quizzing me to get one up on her informants.

"Seems like the level-crossing barrier was left up. La Magnin swears it wasn't, but the facts are there for all to see."

La Magnin—the fat, jaundiced barrier operator. She was from the same area as Mum, on the other side of the Seine. A long time ago she'd shacked up with an old retired pimp and opened up a chip shop on one of the islands round there. Some unkind sorts even said she'd do special favours for generous customers. Her man drowned while poaching pike from the river one winter night, and since the business was in his name she was left without a penny. So she seduced a railway employee, started piling on the weight, and ended up as the barrier operator at Léopoldville.

"It was terrible."

"I knew it," said Mum, walking over to the living-room door to look inside.

"Knew what?"

"That it would end badly. Something told me you should never have come to this house. Now you're out of a job."

I couldn't stand her being so smug and shallow at such a time.

"I won't have you talking like that, Mum! You should be ashamed."

"What?"

"Yes, you should! And anyway, I'm not out of a job. Monsieur Rooland isn't dead."

"You don't think I'm going to leave you here alone with a single man?"

"Why not?"

"How do you mean, 'why not'? A single man's a single man."

You couldn't argue with logic like that. I shrugged.

"What sort of bloke do you think he is? He's a gentleman. D'you think he's going to throw himself straight on top of the maid now his wife's dead?"

"It's a matter of principle."

At that moment, nosing around the kitchen, she didn't seem particularly principled.

"What's that thing there?"

"A blender."

"What's it for?"

"You can use it to make fruit juice, mayonnaise... all sorts."

"What will they think of next! Where are they burying her—here or in America?"

"I don't know."

"Don't you think Monsieur Rooland might go back to his own country now that his wife's dead?"

The idea hadn't even occurred to me, and now it felt like a slap in the face.

"Do you think so?" I blurted, taken aback.

"Well, after the ordeal he's had I should think France might start to get him down... Listen, Louise, if your boss had any old dresses, knick-knacks, well anything at all, really, that you need to get rid of, keep me in mind, will you?"

I didn't answer, but she insisted.

"Will you, Louise?"

"Yes, Mum."

"You're acting all funny, you know."

"Hardly surprising in the circumstances, is it?"

But she carried on.

"You'll never guess what I thought at the beginning."

"The beginning of what?"

"Of this—you working for them."

"What did you think?"

"That there was something going on between you and him, the husband. The way you looked at him, you were all gooey eyed. And then the way he came to hire you himself, all alone... If you ask me..."

She took hold of my arm.

"So I don't want you going back to work for him if he doesn't buzz off to America. You can wait for him to get back from the hospital and give him a hand with arranging the funeral, but after that you have to come home, Louise."

"We'll see," I mumbled.

"You have to, Louise. There's no two ways about it."

Casually, insolently even, she'd opened the pantry and was admiring the pyramids of tins from the NATO headquarters shop.

"American stuff?"

"Yes."

"All of it?"

"All of it."

"Do you think I could take one or two? Just so that Arthur can have a taste."

"I don't think so, Mum."

"What, do they do a stocktake or something?"

"No. *That's* why I don't want you to take any."

That got to her.

"Oh! Louise, you poor thing."

"Why do you say that?"

"It seems to me you've changed, sweetheart. You're not yourself any more."

It seems to me she was right about that.

Eventually she left, but not without reminding me to pack my bags.

The things Mum had said kept nagging away at me. That stuff about me being sweet on Jess worried me. Was it really so obvious that I cared so much for him? Before I'd even admitted its reality to myself, that strange feeling had already escaped from my control and become a weakness, something for other people to prey on.

On top of that, the idea that Monsieur Rooland might leave the country terrified me. Mum was right: it would be a natural next step, given everything that had happened.

I needed to chase away the blues somehow, so I set to tidying the house. For a while longer at least, it belonged to me. I was the new queen of the island.

He came back from the hospital while I was beating the rugs—hardly the ideal moment for him to make his arrival. I was on my hands and knees in the garden with my sleeves rolled up, hitting a doormat, when an ambulance pulled up outside the gate. The man who got out looked like he could've been Jess Rooland's brother, but the resemblance went no further than that. He'd lost weight, which made his face seem longer, and in the daylight you could see that he had bruises all over. It's how I imagine a boxer must look, the day after a fight.

One of his shoulders was all bandaged up, with his jacket draped over the top. His injured leg was stiff as a board inside its iron-wire cast. Jess wouldn't take the arm of the male nurse who was escorting him. He hopped up to the porch on his own, and only then did he steady himself against me with his good arm, while he went up the steps. He nodded a greeting to me. He seemed preoccupied, somehow—a bit rushed, like a man who's just been told he's wanted on the telephone. Once he was in the hall, he let go of me and made his way into the living room, supporting himself against the wall.

The nurse left us, ungraciously. Maybe he was expecting a tip, but Jess didn't think to give him one. He sat down on the sofa where he used to flirt with Madame Rooland.

"I'm very happy to see you back here, Monsieur Rooland…"

Silence. He looked sadly around the room. I wasn't going to let him start staring at the ceiling here too!

"How are you feeling?"

"Eh? What do you say?"

Jess spoke French well, but certain expressions confused him from time to time.

"Are you in pain?"

"Oh! It's nothing."

And then, to my astonishment, he added:

"I had worse when I used to play baseball."

"I wanted to ask you something, Monsieur."

How intelligent his eyes were!

"Are you planning on going back to America?"

"Why do you ask?"

"Well, since Madame…"

"No, Louise. I'll stay."

And just like that it was as if there was music playing inside my head.

He smiled, a smile as weak as he looked.

"My mother was here, Monsieur. She just left."

"Oh?"

"She wanted to give her condolences."

"Thank you."

"And she also wants me to go back to live with her."

I needed to get straight to the heart of the problem. I couldn't have those threats hanging over my head. Better to make a clean breast of it, do whatever was necessary and then I could stop worrying about it.

"Why does she want you to leave here?"

"She says it isn't right for a girl to live with a single man."

"Why not?"

He was certainly frank, Jess Rooland. I wished Mum could've heard him ask that.

"Well, I…"

I was ashamed of myself. Thelma's body wasn't even in the ground, wasn't even in a coffin, and here I was spouting this childish rubbish. There was even hint of hypocritical flirtation in my manner.

"Oh! Yes, I see," sighed Jess.

He stroked his unshaven chin, glinting with the beginnings of a red beard.

"Are you going to do as she tells you?"

"No, Monsieur. I'll stay here as long as you want."

"Well then…"

"But I'm still a minor; if my Mother insists…"

He made a dismissive gesture with his free hand, as if swatting an invisible fly.

"She won't insist. You know very well there's a way to make her see reason."

And he rubbed his thumb and forefinger together, shamelessly.

Cash! They certainly know the power of the dollar, those Americans.

"Thank you," I said, looking down at the floor. "Would you like to go up to bed, Monsieur?"

"No, I have some things to take care of."

"Of course. Is there anything I can help you with?"

"There is. We've got a lot of work to get done, the two of us."

"Will… Will Madame be buried in America?"

"Yes."

"Won't you go to the funeral?"

"No, we'll have a service here, with the NATO chaplain."

He got up with great effort and went over to the record player. It was all set up, ready to play, with a pile of records on the arm. I was shocked for a moment, thinking he was about to turn it on. But instead he took the records and threw them in the fireplace.

"It'll be the same for everything, Louise."

"I don't understand."

"We'll have to get all of my wife's clothes together and give them away."

"All her clothes?"

"Yes, all of them. All her things too, her lingerie… Everything!"

He leant against the chimney, buried his face in the crook of his arm and started talking to himself in English. There was a rhythm to the words, so I think he must have been reciting poetry. It brought tears to my eyes. A sudden sorrow, impossible to hold back. He had a way of being sad that was all his own, did Jess.

THIRTEEN

The police came round in the afternoon as part of their investigations. When I say "the police" I mean the Léopoldville commissioner—the one who'd come to the party and seemed to be so taken with Thelma. The business of the level crossing having been left open was causing a bit of a stink in the town. The Paris newspapers had got hold of the story and were banging on about it, and as you can imagine they were selling well round our way as a result.

What everyone wanted to know was: whose criminal hand had raised the barrier? Because La Magnin wasn't responsible. A couple of station employees, going home at the end of their shifts at around one forty, had testified under oath that the barrier was closed at that time. At one forty-six, though, when the express passed through, it was open. The police decided that some driver in a hurry must have raised the barrier just before the Roolands' arrival and forgotten to put it back down.

Jess received the commissioner in the living room, offering him whisky and a cigar. The policeman sat terribly awkwardly on his chair, his felt hat on one knee. Nothing really important happens round our way, apart from the odd drunken punch-up—that's why they send young coppers out here to get them used to all the paperwork and bureaucracy of the job.

When I left them both, I deliberately kept the door slightly ajar. While I was mopping the hallway floor I could hear every word of their conversation. The commissioner began by offering his condolences, then he got straight down to the facts:

"Monsieur Rooland, could you please tell me everything you remember about your accident, without leaving anything out?"

"That won't take long," Jess replied calmly. "I was driving back from Paris. My wife was asleep… As I was driving across the rails I saw lights to my right. When I realized it was a train… I must have braked. It was an awful moment, commissioner."

"It must have been."

Jess sighed.

"Maybe if I'd stepped on the accelerator we would have been able to get through. I don't know. My foot acted all on its own. It's impossible to control oneself when something like that happens. There was a terribly loud noise. I found myself lying on a pile of stones… And then, well that's all! Do you see?"

"I understand. When you crossed the rails, were you going fast?"

"No. Anyway, I never drive very fast, even on an open road. In the States we have a speed limit, you know?"

"Before you came to the level crossing, were you overtaken by any other vehicles?"

"Yes, by a motorcycle."

"A motorcyclist would have used the gate. He wouldn't have raised the barrier," muttered the commissioner under his breath. "You didn't see the tail lights of another car ahead of you?" he asked Jess.

"No we did not!"

"It's strange. Someone other than the barrier operator turned the crank to raise the barrier before you got there."

"And didn't that fat woman hear a car pull up?"

"No, she was asleep. I turned the crank myself to check—it hardly makes any noise, just a faint clicking… Very good, that'll be all for now, Monsieur Rooland. We'll try to track down the motorcyclist you mentioned. Maybe he'll be able to shed some light on the matter…"

The commissioner left. Jess seemed agitated. He called me in:

"Louise!"

"Monsieur?"

"Have you finished getting all Thelma's clothes together?"

"Yes, Monsieur."

"Who will you give them to?"

That flustered me.

"To my mother—if that's all right with you, of course."

"OK."

"I wanted to ask you, Monsieur—what shall I do with the fur coat? It must be expensive. You could sell it, at least?"

"No, you keep it."

"Me!" I gasped.

"Yes. But I don't want to see you wearing it. Put it to one side for later."

"Oh, Monsieur! What a present—it's too much."

"It's not a present. If you don't want it, give it to anyone you like."

"Oh, well, I'll keep it."

"OK. Now listen, Louise. You'll have to give me your bedroom. You can take mine. I hope you don't mind."

"No, Monsieur."

"Very well, that's all."

*

101

And so Thelma's beautiful fur coat stayed in its cupboard, and I moved into the Roolands' bedroom. I was pleased to have such a gorgeous fur, but unhappy at the thought that that I wasn't to wear it until later. "Later" meant "when I no longer worked for Jess".

If I told you I slept well that evening, in their big upholstered bed, I'd be lying. Apart from anything else, there were people in the house all night—the guests from that party: the general, my overweight dance partner, the French bloke, the Belgian and some others I didn't recognize. They all came round to be with Jess and to comfort him.

To begin with they were solemn and grave, but as the whisky started to flow their voices rose, and I heard them droning on long into the night from my new bedroom. I lay awake until dawn, staring at the bathroom door in the half-light, still expecting to see Thelma walk out dressed in that striped white dressing gown of hers that would sometimes fall aside to reveal a breast or a leg.

The following days passed in a confusing, incoherent blur. There was the service at the NATO chapel, then the departure of the lead-lined coffin in a plane from Orly. As Monsieur Rooland wasn't well enough to drive yet he had an American soldier as his chauffeur—a big, bland, blond guy, who chewed gum instead of making conversation.

As you'd expect, Mum came to visit Jess. She thanked him for the clothes to begin with, then asked him what he planned to do with me. Jess told her unceremoniously that he still needed me, and gave her another twenty thousand francs like you'd throw some change in a beggar's hat. I was ashamed for Mum. I barely recognized the poor woman any more. She was getting greedy with age. If you'd seen her stuffing the notes into her bag I swear it would have sickened you too. When she left I said to Monsieur Rooland:

"I'm ashamed of my mother."

"Why?"

"I feel like she'd agree to anything at all if there was some money in it for her."

He could tell how bitter I was about it and took pity on me.

"No, that's not true. She's never had much money so it makes an impression on her, you're right, but if she's leaving you here it's above all because she understands that I'm a respectable man."

And, believe it or not, those words hurt me more than everything else.

FOURTEEN

We built a new life for ourselves, Jess and me. After a few days
he went back to work, and started coming back to Léopoldville
later and later in the evening. My dinners would often go
uneaten. From that time on, my life was spent waiting. When
he did get home he'd go straight up to bed, sparing me a kind
word as he passed.

One week after it happened he bought a new car: a beautiful
charcoal-coloured Mercury, with grey and coral-pink upholstery, which I'd shine every morning. I still believe he would
have left that house if it wasn't for me, or rather if it wasn't for
the atmosphere that I'd created there—no one will convince
me otherwise. Even so, I could see he wasn't happy there, and
in the evenings the house disturbed him as much as if it were
haunted by Thelma's ghost. Was he really grieving? At first I
was sure he was, but by the second day I was beginning to have
my doubts. You can't imagine how sad it was at the airport,
when they loaded that great big coffin into the belly of that
enormous Pan Am plane. Some of Jess's friends were there,
including the general, in uniform this time. I stood quietly
to the side, alongside the police commissioner. I don't know
why, but it seemed we were the same, him and me—united
by a certain way we had of existing and suffering in silence.

The most moving moment came when the plane took off.
As its engines began to rumble and it moved off towards the
runway, a ripple of tension went through our little gathering.

The general stood to attention. Jess had gone a bit pale, but other than that to look at him he could have been seeing a living Thelma off at the airport. He watched the plane as it rose into the air, and closed his eyes for a second. Then his body hunched over, and for a moment I thought he was going to collapse, but the men around him started to talk and Jess seemed totally relaxed and at ease—relieved, even.

The fine days returned. We had a blazing summer—even a little bit too dry, according to the local farmers. Great clouds of dust twisted in the air behind their tractors as they worked. I must be a funny sort of girl, really. Anyone else my age would've hated the hollow life I was leading, all alone in that big house with the memory of a dead woman, waiting for a man who didn't even look at me—that could get you down in the end, right? Well, not me—I was enchanted by it all. I found all that solitude and silence calming. Despite Jess's coolness, I felt as if he belonged to me somehow, that he was mine and no one else's, and that sooner or later he'd realize it himself. Everything would be possible then. And so, I waited, with a total confidence in the future.

The sun and the warmth reminded me of my first days there. I saw myself in my mind's eye wandering past the house, and I tried to recall how I'd felt the previous year. One afternoon I went out to have a proper look at the place. I leant on the gate for ages, thinking, trying to work out what was missing from this picture of my desert island, because there *was* definitely something missing. In the end I got it: it was the garden swing seat that we'd packed away in the winter and never taken out again.

I ran to the shed. The swing seat was sleeping under a layer of dust. Its blue canopy seemed a little faded, but once I'd given it all a good shake and run the vacuum cleaner over the cushions it looked just as chic as it had the year before, apart from a few bits of rust around the screws. Using a wheelbarrow, I managed to drag it to its old spot by the side of the house. It really was all the place needed to look just as bright and happy as before. I sat on the big swing seat, holding on to the frame.

I thought back to those Sundays with Thelma and Jess. I saw his foot in its white sandal, pushing off from the ground to send the swing gliding through the air, and I could smell his wife's perfume. I don't know where she bought it. It must have come from the US, because you can't buy a fragrance like that in Paris. It smelt of cinnamon and jasmine, and pepper too. I read somewhere that perfumiers add it to their perfumes to give them that extra special something.

But all I could really smell that day, on the swing, was the overpowering scent of lilies. It's a smell that's always reminded me of church. I suppose I think of them as altar flowers. Maybe that's because of one of the statues in our church—of Saint Joseph, holding a bunch of lilies (I don't know why) and looking so embarrassed about it all that I used to laugh to myself all through Sunday school at the awkward look on his face.

I lazed there on the swing for quite a while. I'd rediscovered the island—all in one piece, and even more enchanting, even more mysterious now that Thelma was gone. I had all the time in the world. It was like I was on holiday: I'd finished all my work for the day and Monsieur Rooland wouldn't be back until very late…

Suddenly a familiar noise tore me from my peaceful doze. I sat up to see Jess's car parked outside the gate, which he opened, calling out cheerfully: "Hello, Louise!"

My heart was in my mouth. He hadn't been back this early for months. Did this unexpected arrival mean a change in his feelings? *I've won*, I thought at once. From now on he'd begin to enjoy spending time at the house again. We'd relive all those beautiful evenings I still dreamt of. Just the two of us!

"What a nice surprise, Monsieur!"

"You're going to make us something nice for dinner, OK Louise?"

"OK, Monsieur."

My joy was so intense, so bright, that it hurt, like when you have pins and needles and you know it won't do you any harm, but still your whole body is covered with little pricks of pain.

"Something nice for dinner," he'd said. "Make *us* something nice for dinner"! Oh Jess, my darling Jess...

He was bringing the car in now. I was standing on the drive and I skipped onto the lawn to let him past. That was when I saw her. She was sitting next to him, one elbow on the armrest, just behind the curve of the windscreen, where the reflections stop you from seeing inside properly. She was very beautiful. Much more beautiful than me, of course; much more beautiful than Thelma too! A blonde. A blonde so light her hair was almost white, with haughty, piercing blue eyes.

When she got out of the car I said to myself that she had the prettiest figure I'd ever seen. A model for the swankiest fashion house would have had nothing on her.

I was stunned, standing there on the lawn, rooted to the spot. Jess was smiling. He almost seemed proud of himself. Oh,

God—maybe he even thought this would be a nice surprise for me!

"Come here, Louise…"

I went over, squeezing my thumbs hard enough to crush them inside my clenched fists.

"Hello, Madame."

Jess introduced us, in American, because the girl didn't speak a word of French. I think she said her name was Jennifer. When he said my name she just mumbled "uh-huh"—you know, like they do in a dubbed film when they can't find the right words for the translation.

Jess stopped dead when he noticed the blue swing seat was out. He'd looked at it when he was arriving, but hadn't really taken it in, as you don't when you've seen something so often that it blends into the background.

The sight of it upset him now. It must have reminded him of his evenings with Thelma. And to make matters worse Jennifer headed straight over to it with her magnificent, elegant panther's prowl.

Where on earth had Jess got this pin-up girl from anyway? From the NATO offices? I thought it was only tin cans and cars they flew in from America!

Make us something nice for dinner!

There are times when you could understand a maid spitting in the soup.

I made them a decent meal in the end, though: quiche Lorraine and stuffed veal escalopes, with a chocolate mousse for pudding. From my kitchen I could see everything they got up to, and, believe me, it was enough to turn your stomach.

The girl was playing the vamp, striking poses, pulling faces like you wouldn't believe. I think it was a point of principle with her never to sit without showing off her suspenders, and never to smoke a cigarette without lighting one for a man first.

It was all play-acting—or all movie-acting, more like! Lingering glances. Those *uh-huh*s and the little dabs of the tongue to moisten her lips, making them even more sensual. This well-off widower with his tanned skin and brand-new Mercury must really have caught Jennifer's eye. It was too good an opportunity to let slip through her fingers.

They picked at their food, then went back to the swing seat to take in the dusk: the faint stars in the sky, the breeze and the drunken insects weaving through the air. Jess was giving his conquest little pecks on the neck, making her giggle with pleasure.

Their fingers intertwined. I wondered whether she was going to stay the night. It certainly seemed that way to me. Casually, I went and ran an eye over the car, and saw a little leather suitcase on the back seat. I was right—the little miss was planning on "stopping out", as Arthur called it. I was trembling with anger—with hatred, even. I wanted to make a scene, do something scandalous; anything to set me free, to cure me of this burning pain.

The bonnet of the car was hot. I put my hands flat on the bodywork and stared bitterly at the happy couple through both car windows. Just like the other car's windscreen, the tinted glass gave them an unreal appearance. How romantic the pair of them looked on the swing, cooing at each other. My heartbeat had never been so slow or so strong.

I could see a new happiness for Jess, growing before my eyes with every one of his little fluttering kisses. What could I do about it? Who could tell me how to put a stop to it? Not the good Lord, that was for sure. Maybe Thelma? If there was an afterlife, she couldn't have been happy looking down at this, could she? I put all my effort into thinking of her, asking for her to come to my aid. And, believe it or not, I didn't have to wait long for an answer!

FIFTEEN

It wasn't complicated. But aren't the simplest ideas always the most effective?

I went up to my room. Thelma's record player was there, under my bed, along with her records, which I'd salvaged from the fireplace. When you've grown up somewhere like Arthur's house you don't throw anything away, and coming from where I did I didn't have the luxury of making grand gestures like an American. I also had my late employer's old dressing gown and an almost-full packet of her cigarettes. (Her last!) I got undressed in the blink of an eye and put on the dressing gown, fighting the strange disgust I felt at its touch. I picked up the record player and records and made my way down to the living room, taking a bottle of Scotch from the kitchen along the way.

It was freakish—all of a sudden, I felt as if I really was the reincarnation of Thelma. Mimicking her gestures, striking the same poses as she had done, I felt I was beginning to understand her a little. I was playing at being Thelma. I felt American; I loved drinking and I wanted to stretch out on the sofa, listen to music from back home, and try to forget this strange, alien country, this grey town, and this endless wait for a man I had disappointed by failing to provide him with a child.

Yes, she was with me that evening, Thelma. Even better— she was *in* me.

I plugged in the record player and Elvis Presley's magical voice rose up amid the silence.

> Loving you,
> Just loving you…

The sad, gentle song seemed like a hymn. I lit up a Camel. The tobacco had a sweet taste to it—not bad. I poured myself a glass of whisky. That was more difficult to swallow and I almost lost my "link" with Thelma, but I saw it through and felt the alcohol spark a kind of warm explosion, filling my whole being.

> Loving you…

Couldn't Jess hear? Wasn't he drawn to the music? Or were that little tart's grasping fingers more powerful than the pull of his memory?

The song finished. He wasn't there… I took another slug of Scotch and put the needle back at the beginning of the record.

> Loving you!
> Loving you,
> Just loving you…

The door flew open. Jess stood in the doorway. Seeing me on the sofa, draped in the striped dressing gown with a cigarette between my lips, he closed his eyes, just like at the airport when the aeroplane took off with Thelma's coffin. He hunched over in the same way too.

"Jess," I sighed.

I felt something had snapped inside him. For a moment, I thought he was going to throw himself on me and beat me black and blue, but he shut the door. Presley carried on singing, pointlessly now. After a moment, I heard the soft purr of the car's engine. They were leaving! I drained my glass of whisky and let myself slide into drunkenness.

"Louise!"

I opened my eyes. For a second the room span around the sofa, and then it was still. Jess was standing in the doorway again. If I hadn't remembered the sound of the car leaving, I'd have thought he'd never moved.

The light on the record player, which I'd left plugged in, cast a reddish glow in the darkened room. Its motor was droning away.

"Louise!"

He came into the room. There was a hardness to his features that I'd never seen before.

"Louise!"

"Yes, Monsieur!"

"Why did you do this dreadful thing?"

My tongue was sticking to the roof of my mouth. I could hardly speak.

"Has she left?"

"I took her back to her place, yes. Well?"

"What did you tell her?"

"It doesn't matter what I told her. Answer the question! What's the meaning of this performance you've put on?"

"I didn't want her to stay."

"You don't say!"

I lifted a leg. The dressing gown fell back, exposing bare flesh. It was the first time in my life I'd felt a physical hunger for a man.

"Jess!"

I held out my arms to him.

"Jess!" I groaned again.

"Get up. Go to your room…"

But there was a note in his voice that no girl could mistake, not even a virgin. I felt a sudden urge to grab hold of his jacket. I caught hold of the cloth and pulled him towards me in a wild, feminine gesture.

"Jess! Oh! Jess…"

He fell to his knees by the sofa and, at long last, he crushed his lips against my own.

What happened next, I couldn't tell you if my life depended on it. You try to put ecstasy into words, if you can!

SIXTEEN

We each slept in our own bedroom in the end, but just afterwards we went upstairs together, and Jess had his arm around my waist.

When we reached the landing he kissed me like a madman, pressing my body against his. Unsteady on my feet, I opened the door to my room, by which I mean "their" room. I thought he was going to follow me, but when I turned around he'd already disappeared into his own. I shut my door gently, and slid between the white sheets, quivering with pleasure.

My body was burning, bruised and happy. Falling asleep feeling like that was just stretching out the pleasure Jess had given me.

When you shake the grille of a central-heating furnace, the sound travels through the whole house because of the pipes. I recognized that sound when it woke me up the next morning. It worried me straight away, because I'm usually the first to get up, and we hadn't lit the central heating for a couple of months.

What was Monsieur Rooland doing in the cellar at this time in the morning? In my hurry to go and find out, I wanted to put on the dressing gown from the night before, but it wasn't in my bedroom any more. This new mystery only added to my unease. I flung my dress on with nothing underneath, shoved my feet into a pair of old red slippers and hurtled down the stairs. A horrible burning smell was rising from under the floorboards. Bursting into the coal cellar I found Jess in his blue pyjamas, stamping angrily on the record player, breaking it to pieces.

"Jess!"

But he didn't even look up. Sweat poured down his face as he trampled the turntable under his feet. It must have been hurting him—he wasn't wearing shoes, just his usual sandals.

The furnace door was open, the inside ablaze. In the flickering light of the flames I could see the dressing gown and several records, all shrivelled up, like those mushrooms people leave to dry at their windows in the countryside.

"What are you doing?"

As if in answer, he gathered up the remains of the record player in his hands. It looked like some poor animal that had been squashed at the side of a road, its guts all hanging out. Jess threw it in the furnace and wiped his dripping face with his sleeve.

"Why did you do that, Jess?"

"I didn't want it any more."

What didn't he want any more? What was he trying to get rid of? His memories of Thelma, or of our lovemaking? I threw myself against his heaving chest.

"Jess, my dear."

He took me by the shoulders and pushed me away firmly, murmuring: "No, Louise, *sorry*!"

"But Jess!"

"No, it's quite out of the question. I'm extremely sorry about last night. I'm afraid I lost my head."

So, that was all our night was to him. He'd lost his head!

"But I love you, Jess. I've always loved you, since the first day I saw you. That's why I came to ask you to take me on, you know that!"

He shook his head.

"You're a little girl, Louise."

"Not any more!" I shouted. "Not any more, you American pig!"

"Don't say that, Louise, you remind me of…"

"Of who?…"

"No…"

"Say it!"

"Of your mother!"

"Oh! Jess…"

I'd pulled away from him, and this time it was Jess who put his arms around me. I was allowed to rest my head on his chest again. His sweat ran down my cheek. I could hear his heart thumping.

"You don't love me?"

"No, Louise."

"You prefer that girl from last night?"

"No, not her either!"

"Why did you bring her here?"

"Oh! To take my mind off things… Men are like that, Louise. Lots of adventures, but only one love."

"And who is your love? Thelma?"

"Yes."

I would never have believed such a thing. Jess in love with his wife! But he seemed to have taken her death so easily. I didn't know what else to say. I could see that he was telling the truth, that he felt sorry for me and that this scene was painful for him.

"What will I do?" I sobbed.

Everything was finished. The desert island was sinking under the Léopoldville soot. I saw Ridel's factory, Arthur's telly, our grimy lampshade, and Mum with her bloody harelip, counting out lumps of sugar to see how many there were in a kilo.

The day I came here for the first time Jess had told me that my seventeen years were worth four hundred million dollars; I was ready to give them up for much less than that, ready to let them go for free if I had to.

"So, Monsieur Rooland, what am I going to do now?"

"You're young!"

Well, there you go! I'd certainly heard that one before.

So I was young. All right, but so what? Wasn't that exactly my problem? Having a youth that I didn't know what to do with. A youth that was withering away under dirty grey skies. A youth that the man I love took advantage of one evening when he... when he lost his head, and then rejected me the next morning.

That burning dressing gown and trampled record player summed it up—a disaster.

"You can shove my youth in the furnace while you're at it, Monsieur Rooland!"

"Let's go upstairs," he said.

The fire crackled softly, already beginning to die down. I followed Jess up to the ground floor. The sun had risen while we were in the cellar, and was beginning to shine through the gaps in the blinds. The living room, where I had been so madly happy the previous evening, was now bathed in violet shadow.

I looked at it incredulously. I couldn't believe that I had been Jess's mistress the previous evening, and that everything was over already. I told myself that if I'd only spent the night in his arms, he'd never have dared to act like that in the morning. It all would have played out differently. Now, though, it was too late. Too late!

"Explain it to me, Monsieur Rooland."

"Explain what?"

"This love for your wife. I still don't understand!"

He poured himself a glass of Scotch. The bottle was lying on the threadbare carpet.

"You won't ever understand, Louise."

"You don't think so?"

"We never understand other people's loves…"

"Madame explained some things to me, though."

"What things?"

"The child you wanted and that she couldn't give you. She said that your life together was like a walk in the woods in winter."

"She said that?"

"Yes. You see, what I still don't get is why you cared for her so much: a drunk! A tart!"

He threw himself on me and shook me so violently that my head hit the wall.

"I forbid you! I forbid you, Louise!"

And he carried on saying things in English that he was too angry to translate.

"Let me go, Monsieur Rooland! You're hurting me," I cried. That proved that everything was really over between us. He was "Monsieur Rooland" to me now, not Jess any more.

"I'll go," I stammered. "That is what you want now, isn't it?"

He shook his head, defeated by my reasonable tone.

"No. Stay… I just want it to be like it was before."

"Your servant? Just your servant, right?"

"OK!"

He went upstairs to take his bath. When he left an hour later, without saying goodbye, I wondered whether I'd ever see him again.

SEVENTEEN

He stayed away for forty-eight hours. I couldn't possibly describe to you what it was like: that night I spent all alone on the island, waiting for the sound of his step on the sand driveway.

As the hours passed, all the anger I'd felt towards him faded away. Little by little I was forgetting that morning's scene, and thinking instead about the endless love he had given me the night before. He'd regretted "losing his head" afterwards, but, in the moment, I knew he'd been as completely happy as me. Thinking it over, I began to tell myself that his fury in the cellar could almost be taken as a sign of his love for me. If he'd spent the night with that Jennifer there wouldn't have been any fit of anger afterwards. He wouldn't have destroyed the turntable or the dressing gown, because her embraces would have meant nothing to him. So, with me, it had been different. I had to console myself with that thought.

The next day, at nine o'clock, I called NATO headquarters to get some news. They passed me from department to department until I reached his, and I recognized his voice. His dear, dear voice.

His accent sounded stronger on the telephone.

"Yes, hello."

"Is that you, Monsieur?"

"Oh! Louise…"

"I'm sorry, I just wanted to know…"

I hung up. He was alive, what did the rest matter? I couldn't care less if he'd spent the night with his fake blonde. Actually that girl was worth a night, two maybe, but no more.

And in the end, Jess came back alone that evening... came home. It was as if he was returning from a long journey. We spent an emotional moment looking each other up and down, closely, as if each of us was trying to see how the other had changed.

"Hello, Louise."

"Yes."

"Why did you hang up the phone this morning? Were you angry?"

"No, happy. I was so afraid that..."

"That what?"

"I don't know. When you're properly afraid it's hard to put into words. What do you want for dinner?"

"It doesn't matter."

We opened the tins. The Thelma method. I had to admit, it had its merits. I'd been chipping away at the stocks in the cupboard for some time myself. Grubby towels had started to reappear on the shower head, there were hairs in the soap and the furniture was getting dusty too. It's not so bad when all's said and done, dust. Time's notebook. You can write all sorts of silly things in it with your fingertip—things like, "I love you, Jess". You can draw hearts, like lovers carve on tree trunks... Or intertwined initials. J.-L. Jess-Louise. Monsieur Rooland didn't notice this slide into mess and uncleanliness. There are lots of things men don't notice. It's as if their eyes can only see the big picture. The details pass them by.

We ate our meal at the kitchen table because a bad wind was blowing factory soot into the garden. Everything this side of the Seine gets covered in black grime; on the other side it's a dirty white, thanks to all the cement works and quarries.

We ate facing each other. Monsieur Rooland hadn't changed for dinner. He was wearing his brown linen suit with a white shirt, open to show his tanned chest, and black-and-tan-coloured shoes. We had nothing to say to each other, but funnily enough the silence didn't weigh heavily. It didn't bother me, anyway.

After dinner, Jess listened to the radio in the living room while I half-heartedly soaped the dishes in the kitchen. He was listening to an English station, I think. Unusually for him, he didn't drink any whisky. When I'd finished I found him sitting on a chair the wrong way round, his arms resting on the back, a cigarette in his lips. He stared at the radio, squinting through the smoke; I didn't dare talk to him. Sitting like that, it was obvious Jess was mulling over an important decision. That might be a good thing for me, I thought.

I lay down on the sofa and gazed at him tenderly. If you only knew how handsome he was there, motionless, his cleft chin resting on the back of his hand. He might have been a painting. I could have happily spent the rest of my days admiring him. But, after a while, the music cut out and an announcer's voice started jabbering away, reading the news. I caught the names of politicians and countries. Jess didn't give a toss about current affairs. He got up and switched the radio off. The sudden silence shocked me out of my dreamy state.

"Good night, Louise."

"Monsieur."

Without even looking at me, he stubbed his cigarette out in a marble ashtray and went up the stairs. I waited a while, telling myself that he'd change his mind. I'd been waiting in hope for the night. Men think differently once the shadows fall; they listen to the secret voices that whisper inside them. But I heard him taking a shower, and then the squeaking of his bed springs as he climbed between the sheets. I was afraid in the living room now. I felt even more alone than I had when Monsieur Rooland wasn't in the house. Quickly sliding the bolt on the front door and turning the gas off, I went upstairs too. I felt a strange sickness in my bones.

It was as if I had the flu coming on, but that wasn't it really. Once I was undressed, my nightgown in my hand, I saw my body in the wardrobe mirror and I understood. This was Thelma's sickness. Wasn't it to cure herself of it that she came up here and stripped off in the evenings, that she purred and rubbed herself up against Jess like a cat in heat?

My nightgown fell to my feet. Mechanically, I opened my door and rushed the two metres across the landing to his. Jess hadn't locked it.

He was reading an American tabloid newspaper. It fell to the floor when I burst into the room. He glanced anxiously at my naked body and I panicked. I flung my hand desperately at the light switch. Then the dark cured me of my sudden shyness and everything was simple again.

I didn't leave him that evening. I stayed pressed up against him, savouring his manly body heat. At one point, long after the lovemaking, I thought I heard a stifled laugh. I put my hand up to his lips to check: I was right, he was laughing.

"What is it?"

"Do you know what I'm thinking about, Louise? About your mother. She guessed this would happen. Quite something, isn't it?"

"Not really. She saw from the beginning that I was in love with you."

"Is that true?"

"She told me."

"When you're back at her place, will you tell her about my ungentlemanly conduct?"

When you're back at her place!

I leapt out of bed and rushed over to the light switch, fighting against the darkness as desperately as I'd fought against the light on coming into the room.

"Why do you say that I'll go back to her place?"

He blinked, surprised by my reaction.

"It's inevitable, Louise!"

"Inevitable?"

"Of course. And I'll go back to the USA."

I was impressed by my own calm. All of a sudden I was filled with a sort of detached acceptance. When they put men in front of a firing squad they must feel that same supreme indifference. That must be what allows them to die well.

"When are you leaving?"

"In a week, maybe two. It depends on my bosses, but I've submitted my request…"

"When…"

"Yesterday."

"Why are you leaving?"

I could have been asking him to fill out a form. My voice was bland, almost bureaucratic.

"Because I need her, Louise," he sighed, turning his head away.

He stared up at the ceiling, like on the night of the accident, when the old nun told him that Thelma was dead.

"What's waiting for you in America? A grave?"

"Memories too. We met in New Orleans. There's a road, down there, near the lake… A great big highway, lined with motels and gas stations, leading up to the state of Mississippi. It certainly isn't beautiful, with its electricity pylons and its used-car lots. But it means more to me than the Champs-Elysées because that's where I met Thelma. Do you see?"

I saw, but I didn't care. So, Thelma still wasn't truly dead, even now!

"Don't you want to take me with you?"

Not only had he never asked himself the question before— the idea seemed to shock him, like it was inappropriate even to suggest such a thing.

"Oh! No, Louise."

"Please. I'm begging you!" I whispered.

"There's no way!"

For him, that night was nothing like the first. I wasn't a young girl any more, offering herself to him in all her innocence, and shamelessness too. I was just a piece of skirt to share his bed with now. A notch on the bedpost, nothing more than a Jennifer!

I got up and let him have it, spitting venom, my hands clenched tightly on the bedstead. He could see me in the harsh glare of the light bulb now, but I didn't give a damn. Monsieur Rooland could gawp all he wanted.

"You're nothing but a creep," I hurled at him. "Do you think I'm going to buy all that romantic rubbish? All your happy memories of the good old days? I know what that's all about."

He was caught off guard by my unexpected attack. He drew back, pulling his knees up under the sheets—afraid all of a sudden, like a naughty kid who's just realized how far he's overstepped the mark.

"You aren't going back there for love, Monsieur Rooland. Do you want me to tell you the real reason? Guilt! *The guilt of having killed your wife!*"

It was incredible how old he seemed all of a sudden. Perhaps it was because he was hunched up in the bed like that, but whatever it was he looked ten years older.

"Louise!"

It was more of a plea for mercy than a reproach.

"Because you killed Thelma, admit it!"

"Louise!" he cried, the pitch of his voice rising. "Louise, that is an utterly appalling thing to say!"

"And it's utterly true too."

"No! No!"

"Yes! You killed her because you caught her with that white-haired bloke in the car. Worse than the lowest tart, Monsieur Rooland. Do you know what a tart is, Monsieur Rooland? It's another word for a whore. That's what your wife was: a real whore. So you killed her. No wonder they couldn't find whoever it was supposedly raised the barrier at the level crossing. You turned the crank yourself! Thelma was asleep in the passenger seat. You left your car on the rails and set yourself up on the embankment to enjoy the show!"

I was picturing it all in my head, telling the story as if from memory, picking out all the details… Since that night, I'd been playing the film of the "accident" over and over in my head. I'd seen the truth of what happened in Thelma's eyes when she'd woken up in the ambulance. That's what she would have told me if death hadn't stopped her.

"I don't know how you managed to hurt yourself. Perhaps you didn't do it on purpose. Maybe you just got hit by a bit of debris or something. Anyway, it wasn't an accident, it was murder. You killed your wife! You killed your wife!"

I was screaming myself hoarse. I could taste blood in my mouth.

Monsieur Rooland leapt out of the bed and grabbed me roughly round the waist. I kicked and struggled like a madwoman, thinking he was about to kill me too. He threw me onto the bed and I fell awkwardly, my head hanging over the edge of the mattress. He would only have had to press down on my face to break my neck. I smiled:

"Go on, then! Murder me too to shut me up."

He let me go, but didn't move away from me. His tanned skin glowed, as if lit up by his inner fury.

"You're a horrible little liar."

"You killed her!"

"If you say that once more I swear I will crush you like a disgusting spider."

"You killed her!"

He buried his face in his hands. I could hear words escaping from between the fingers. English words. I felt sorry for him.

"Jess... Listen, it doesn't change my love for you. I understand why you did it. It'll be our secret. We won't tell a soul. Not a soul!"

Was he even listening? I stopped. The sound of wind blowing in the trees rose up from the garden. The swing seat squeaked like a rusty weathervane. He let his hands fall.

"Where did you get this shameful idea from, Louise?"

I had to keep on going, all the way to the end, if I was going to get what I wanted.

"It's not just an idea, Monsieur Rooland. Madame told me the truth in the ambulance."

"No!"

"Yes!"

He went over to the chest of drawers and took something out of the bottom drawer. For a second I was worried, thinking it might be a revolver. But it was just a black book, with golden letters emblazoned on the spine: HOLY BIBLE.

"This is my wedding Bible," Jess said solemnly. "Do you swear, on this holy book, that my wife really made such an accusation against me before she died?"

That sent a shiver down my spine. Could I really swear to that? Thelma hadn't actually said anything to me, it was just her eyes...

"I swear it!"

He put the Bible down on the bedside table. How ridiculous it all must have looked. This man in his pyjamas, asking a naked girl to swear on a Bible! I feel ashamed to think of it now, and not because of my lie—because of how childish Jess's behaviour was, in the middle of such dramatic scene.

"What did she say exactly?"

I had sudden a flash of inspiration. I gave him the words in English. When Thelma was still alive and I came to their dinner table to ask which one of them wanted the ketchup or the mustard, she'd always murmur something like "'ts Jess".

"Answer me, Louise. What did my wife tell you?"

He didn't seem angry any more. Far from it—he was like a whipped dog.

"She said "ts Jess'."

"And then?"

That wouldn't do him. He was expecting a direct accusation.

"And then she said…"

At that moment, I had no idea what I was going to say. But inspiration always comes to the rescue when you need to tell a dirty lie.

"And then she said, in French this time: 'He wanted me dead. He wanted me dead!'"

I'll never forget what happened next. Jess cried out at the top of his voice—a groan like the splintering of a tree trunk, falling to earth after the last blow of the logger's axe. A terrifying sound. One day, if you're going at a hundred miles an hour in your car and you realize the brakes aren't working, maybe you'll make a sound like that too. Everyone who sees their death coming makes that awful sound—either out loud or in their head.

"Monsieur Rooland!"

He pulled me off of the bed and threw me out of the room. The door slammed shut behind me. I found myself on the darkened landing. I tried the handle, but he'd drawn the bolt this time. I dropped to my knees.

Despite my nakedness, I didn't feel the cold of the night.

With my cheek up against the bottom of the door, I whispered:

"Jess, don't push me away… I told you, it doesn't matter. You were right to leave your car on the rails like that… She only got what she deserved. She was a whore, Jess… Nothing but a whore! Keep me, Jess. I'll love you for ever. I'll never be with anyone apart from you! Never!"

He didn't answer. I stayed there for hours, talking to the ray of yellow light shining through the crack under his door.

EIGHTEEN

I suppose I must have gone back to my room at some point. I don't remember a thing about it. I don't remember falling asleep either, that is, if you can call it sleep—more like a numbing of my brain from sorrow and regret.

I remember listening out in vain for Jess, trying to hear what he was up to, but all I heard were the wild gusts of wind in the garden.

When I came to, in the sad, unforgiving light of day, the awfulness of the situation was clear to me. There was no more sun. The house was no desert island any more—it was just another part of my sad, grey town now.

From now on I'd live inside that artist's painting—the one who came and sat behind our garden that time, to paint the saddest picture in the whole wide world.

I shouldn't have told Jess that I knew. He'd done it, of course, but so long as nobody knew about it he can't have felt truly guilty.

Now it would never be the same. Somebody knew! And because somebody knew, he'd become a murderer for real.

It was eight o'clock, according to my alarm clock. Normally I would have been up well before that time, but I didn't have the energy to get out of bed, get dressed and go down to the kitchen. I think I must have had a fever too. I was shivering and my chest burned when I breathed too deeply.

I lay there in bed. The silence in the house worried me. There were no noises coming from his bedroom. At last, at half-past eight, I heard the shower splutter into life. He'd got up a bit late, but he was going through his usual morning routine.

He probably thought I was busy making him his coffee and fried eggs, like every other morning.

Shortly after that he went downstairs. I listened closely, following his movements about the house. He went into the kitchen.

He was hardly in there for a second—just long enough to give his shoes a quick brush. He could give breakfast a miss for once.

Then he left. Was he really going to go without seeing how I was first? It was as if he had a thread tied around his waist—a long thread, and I was holding the other end. Jess could go as far away as he wanted, to the end of the world, even—that thread would still join him to me, without him having the faintest idea that it was there.

The squeaking of the gate, the purring of the car's engine, the heavy clunk of the driver's door… He was leaving all right. Sod it, it didn't matter. I pulled the sheets up to my nose to enjoy the full effect of my fever. Sometimes it feels good just to lie and sweat in a stiflingly hot bed—it felt like my final refuge.

Imagine if I was on an Arctic ice floe, floating south. As the temperature rose, the ice floe would melt. Well, the Rooland ice floe had melted—all that remained were these three metres of mattress, on which I could float a little bit longer before I found myself in the sea.

The purring of the car's engine, the heavy clunk of the driver's door, the squeaking of the gate. No doubt about it: Jess had come back!

He was wearing a suit I hadn't seen before: with thick purple and blue stripes. A purple shirt. Like a bunch of lilacs. Except he gave off an air of sadness. An air of mourning.

He was wearing a hat—a straw hat, as usual, with a ribbon that was too big.

"Why don't you get up?"

"I'm ill!"

He put his hand on my forehead. His touch felt wonderful. It was worth a thousand cold compresses.

"Do you want me to call a doctor?"

"No!"

He wasn't really interested. He hadn't come back to see how I was—he wanted to ask me some questions, and he got straight to the point.

"Louise, you lied to me."

"Leave me alone."

"My wife can't have told you that I let the crash happen on purpose. She was sleeping when the accident happened!"

"She must have woken up at the last moment. It wouldn't have taken long to understand what was happening."

"You swore that you were going to tell the truth, Louise."

"And I'll swear it again, Monsieur Rooland. Even in court, if I have to!"

He nodded his head. The dimple in his chin was deeper than ever.

"Monsieur Rooland…"

"Yes?"

"You know, you have to take me to America. You have to! Don't worry, I won't get in the way. I'll do the housework, and even if you bring other girls home, even if you get married again, I'll never breathe a word to anyone."

"No!"

"But Monsieur Rooland, I can't live apart from you. I only want one thing: to see you. To cook your meals, make your coffee…"

"In the States, men in my position don't have maids, Louise."

"So I'll find another job near you!"

He cut me short:

"I may never go back to the USA, Louise."

"My God, really?"

"Yes."

"You're not just saying that, for my sake?"

"No. Tell me, are you really sure that Thelma…"

Her again! I was sick of Thelma.

"…that Thelma said those words? You're sure you heard her correctly?"

"I'm not deaf. And if you'd seen her eyes, Monsieur Rooland… They were shooting flames. You're lucky she's dead, otherwise she would have told the police what you did and you'd be in prison now."

He was stunned. He repeated what I'd said, as if he was trying to make sense of it.

"Lucky that she's dead!"

"That's right."

"Thelma would never have accused me of…"

"But she did."

"She was delirious, Louise, she was just delirious…"

"No, Monsieur Rooland, she wasn't delirious, she knew what was going on. She wanted revenge, if you ask me."

"Thelma didn't hold grudges. Even if she did think it was my fault, she wouldn't have wished me ill."

"And what would you know about it? Do you know what it's like to be on your deathbed? When you can feel your life slipping away, and you know it's your husband's fault... of course you bloody well wish him ill!"

He sat down on the edge of the bed, one of my feet underneath him. It hurt my ankle a bit, but I didn't budge an inch. I liked to feel his weight pressing down on me. It gave me the feeling that he would always be there.

"If you knew how much I love you, Monsieur Rooland."

I would have liked to call him Jess, like I had on that first evening, but I couldn't any more.

My declaration left him cold.

"So, Thelma died thinking that I'd killed her," he said, lost in thought.

It didn't make any sense. Instead of worrying himself sick over the threat I was to him, all he could think about was Thelma.

"So what? What difference does it make?" I cried out. "She's dead. She can't accuse you any more. There's only one person you need to worry about, Monsieur Rooland: me!"

He leant towards me. I hoped he was going to kiss me, but then I saw the empty, glassy look in his eyes.

"*You!* You're a snake, Louise."

"Monsieur Rooland!"

"A snake that bites anyone who comes too close."

"And you're a murderer. All this talk about your love for Thelma—don't make me laugh! If you loved her, would you have got rid of all her things? Would you have brought a girl back here? Would you have taken advantage of me? There's nothing in your heart, Jess Rooland. You don't love anyone.

You made your wife unhappy, and when all's said and done maybe it's because of you that she ended up a slut."

Jess stood up.

I'll never forget the way he looked: the grimace on his face, the two furrows above his desperate eyes, his sagging shoulders.

I slid out of bed and wrapped my arms around his legs.

He took hold of my chin and tipped my head back.

"Did Thelma die thinking that I killed her, Louise?"

I thought I was going mad.

"Yes!" I screamed. "Yes! Yes! *Yes!*"

He left.

NINETEEN

Rather than going back to my bed, I went to Jess's. The sheets were cold, but they reminded me of our previous night's love-making. And they had that Rooland smell, a manly, tobacco-tinged scent that tugged at my heart.

I curled up in a ball, hugging the pillow to my chest with both arms, whispering Jess's name to it. I was used to lying like that. I may as well admit it now: I'd done the same every night since I'd arrived on the island.

After a while, I felt something cold and smooth against my hand, an uncomfortable feeling. Looking down, I saw it was a photo. A photo of Thelma, but a Thelma ten or so years younger than I'd known her, with long hair and a fuller face, beaming with happiness. The photograph had been taken on an American street. I could see some black people in the background, and a policeman too, in a peaked hat, with all sorts of equipment hanging off his belt.

So, Jess had gone to sleep looking at this photograph?

Despite the laughter in her eyes, there was a watchfulness to Thelma's gaze, somehow. It gave me a funny feeling, like she was really *looking* at me, if you know what I mean? She was looking at me like she had in the ambulance, trying to make sense of something about me, something that isn't clear.

And suddenly I understood.

"Listen, Thelma," I stammered, "it's true, I think—you're the only one he loves. If he set up that accident it was out of

141

love, only out of love, because of your fooling around with that general. He couldn't get that image out of his head, do you see? But he'll love you until his dying day. I was wrong to carry on like I did, wrong to want him for myself at any price. You're stronger than me; you win. I'm just a common kid from Léopoldville who got carried away. The factory, Arthur's house—that's where I belong… If people like me want a grand, romantic affair we can watch it in the cinema or on the telly. Fields of cabbages, washing yourself standing up at the sink, mopeds coughing out filthy blue smoke—that's what our lives are made of. Forgive me, Thelma. Forgive me. When Jess comes back I'll tell him the truth, all right? You didn't say anything to me. Nothing! I saw it in your eyes, that's all. I could have been wrong. I'll tell him everything, I promise.

"After that he can think about you as much as he wants, about that highway in New Orleans that goes to the state of Mississippi. By the way, how did you end up meeting on a road like that?"

The photograph was soaked with my tears now, the image blurring rapidly. And so Thelma died peacefully in my hands—satisfied, it seemed to me.

Now I couldn't wait for Jess to come back, for him to give me his Bible so that I could… *unswear*. When I was little, if anyone (rightly) doubted what I was saying, I would swear to them that it was true, but in secret I was crying out "I unswear! I unswear it for you, baby Jesus!"

A knock on the front door woke me up. I'd fallen asleep on Madame's photograph. The rectangle of paper was all crumpled and torn.

I went to look out of the window and saw the police commissioner on the doorstep.

"I'm coming!" I cried.

I was trembling so much I didn't even manage to put my dress on.

He seemed taken aback when I opened the door. I can't have been a pretty sight: unwashed, sickly, my hair all over the place, my face all puffy from crying, my bare feet shoved into a pair of tatty old slippers.

"I'm sorry, I… I was in bed. I've got the flu."

"Oh! I'm afraid I'm disturbing you."

He was being tactful. I could tell he thought I'd been upstairs with my employer.

"I'd like to speak to Monsieur Rooland."

"He's not here."

I saw a weary scepticism in his eyes.

"What a pity. When will he be back?"

"It depends, but if it's something urgent you can always call him at NATO headquarters."

This time he believed me, finally.

"I have some news for him regarding our investigation. We've arrested the people responsible."

It was like a hammer blow to the back of my skull.

"Which people?" I stammered.

"The ones who raised the level-crossing barrier on the night of the accident. A couple of soldiers on leave. Drunk. Raised the barrier for a laugh. Unfortunately their stupid prank had tragic consequences…"

The rest became a background hum. I'd stopped listening. I caught the odd phrase here and there.

"Under arrest... brought before the court..."

The young commissioner wasn't paying much attention to his words any more either. I'd bet anything that he'd thought Jess was guilty, just like me.

The image of Thelma and the general in the car that night, dazed and blinking in the light, must have stayed with him, tormented him. He probably fancied Thelma himself—enough to imagine how her husband might feel, enough to understand his need for revenge... So now he was relieved to have got to the bottom of it all. He'd gone after the culprits—doggedly, methodically—and he'd found them.

"...You really don't seem well, I won't bother you any further..."

I was seeing everything through a thick fog.

"Could you please ask Monsieur Rooland to stop by my office?"

I must have nodded, or said something in response. He raised a finger to his cap in salute and his thin figure disappeared back down the drive.

In every home, even Arthur's, there's a sort of warm vibration in the air that comes from the people living there. No sooner had I shut the front door than the Roolands' house became a cold, dead thing, like a switch somewhere had been flicked to "off". A feeling of foreboding came over me. The furniture looked as if it had been slumbering under dust sheets for an age. The floorboards smelt of mould.

I went over to the telephone. Would it still work? Lifting up the receiver I heard the familiar crackle, but rather than feeling relief at this sign of life, I found myself thinking of the vastness of the skies above, teeming with worlds upon worlds.

I dialled the number for NATO headquarters. I had to let Jess know as soon as possible, to tear him from the nightmare I'd plunged him into. They connected me to his office, where a girl asked me who I was. I told her I was Monsieur Rooland's maid. It gave me a jolt to hear myself say it. His maid! Yes, that's all I was, just a maid: somebody who does the dishes, shines the shoes and scrubs the floors, not somebody who acts out an epic romance novel with her employer.

"What is the reason for your call?"

The girl on the end of the line had an American accent, stronger than Jess's.

"I'd like to speak with Monsieur."

"With which Monsieur?"

"My Monsieur, of course! Monsieur Rooland."

"He's not here at the moment."

She certainly had a piercing voice, this secretary. Perhaps it was because of her bad French. Maybe she didn't trust the words she was saying to get her meaning across.

"As soon as he arrives in the office, can you tell him to call the house?"

"Yes."

"Don't forget, it's very important."

Her answer to that was to hang up.

I did the same, blindly fumbling to put the phone back on the hook as I stared into space, lost in thought. I could feel the blood pounding in my temples. The shivers running through my body were coming more and more quickly now. I went and took some aspirin. I had to get rid of this flu. I was going to need all my strength to tell Jess the truth. How could I ever own up to a lie like this?

I didn't have the strength to look into his solemn child's eyes, to see his contempt for me in them. I wouldn't be able to go on after that.

I didn't know what to do with myself. I was in a terrible state. I'd chopped down a tree only to have it fall on top of me.

Maybe I'd find a bit of peace and quiet upstairs? The darkened bedrooms behind their closed shutters seemed much less threatening than the ground floor.

I went back to Jess's bedroom. On the bedside table, the Bible's golden lettering glistened like the wings of a bee in the sun. Fearfully, I took the fat black book in my hands. The rough leather of the cover unsettled me, as if it were a living skin.

HOLY BIBLE.

Did Jess really believe all the barbaric things written in there? On the first page there was a cross, with an English sentence written above it. Did that mean our God was an American too? And people prayed to him in these words, which I didn't even understand? I'd sworn a lie on these flimsy pages, decorated with their Gothic capital letters.

Was that as bad as if I'd sworn a false oath on a French Bible? What did "Holy Bible" mean exactly? Maybe it wasn't the same Bible as ours? One thing was the same: that cross, shaded so that it seemed to stand out from the page. The telephone rang. The sound seemed to come from very far away. It had to be Jess calling me back. Would I have to make my confession over the telephone?

What was it he'd called the black book? "My wedding Bible"? So they had a special Bible for getting married in America?

The telephone's nagging ring was still there, screaming in

146

the silence of the house. With every trill of the bell I shook my head, murmuring: "No, Jess! I don't dare. No, Jess!"

It was worse than if he'd been there in front of me, with his tanned skin and that expectant look on his face.

I tried to hold out, but the ringing wouldn't stop. Finally, I went downstairs, the Bible clutched against my chest.

I don't know if you've ever had occasion to stare at a telephone while it rings and rings, crying at you to answer it. Well I have, and take it from me, it feels horrible. It's as if your whole destiny is crammed into that little plastic box, calling out to you for help. I was hoping that the ringing would stop. Once it was silent again, I'd have the time to conquer my fear before calling back.

"Hello!"

I snatched up the handset and held it to my ear. The secretary's cold, impatient voice drilled into my skull.

"Is this Mister Rooland's maid speaking?"

"His maid, yes."

"Mister Rooland is back in the office now. He'd like to know what you wanted to talk to him about."

I didn't understand. Why didn't Jess want to speak to me himself? Was it really over, then? The sound of my voice was repulsive to him now, even on the telephone...

"Could you please just put him on?" I begged.

"Mister Rooland is busy. He said you should speak to me."

"Let me speak to him! It's very important!"

"One moment, please."

He must have been standing in front of her. She explained my insistence to him in their language. I couldn't hear a reply, but he must have shaken his head.

"Mister Rooland can't speak to you. Would you like to tell me the reason for your call or not?"

She was a stubborn mule all right, this girl. As upset as I was, I found myself conjuring up her image: flat-chested, bucktoothed, and I'd give you ten to one she had an awful name too.

"Would you please tell Monsieur Rooland that the police came to the house? He should go to the Léopoldville commissioner's office as soon as possible."

Why did I get the feeling that Jess had picked up a second receiver? All of a sudden I could sense his presence on the line.

"Are you listening, Monsieur Rooland?" I cried. "No! Don't hang up, I beg you, go to the commissioner's office before you come home. They'll explain everything to you, I don't think I could bear it…"

Just then, the Bible slipped from my grasp. I tried to catch it, but clumsily pressed the hook on the telephone in doing so. When I put the receiver to my ear again, all I could hear was the maddening hiss that made me think of the great empty skies above.

The aspirin was doing its job. I was feeling a bit better. Not completely better, but at least well enough to get on with my daily chores.

I had to get back to work: vacuum the living room, then the bedrooms. I only had a few hours in which to become a good little maid again. If I could somehow curl up into my shell, maybe it would make the dreaded confrontation with Monsieur Rooland a little easier to bear.

It would be easier for both of us if all he had to do was get rid of an employee, rather than a lover. Mum always says, the bigger they are the harder they fall. It may be just a stale old saying, but there's some truth in it. Take it from me.

TWENTY

Rather than making me drowsy and sluggish, the fever seemed to give me a boost. I don't remember ever working as hard as I did that afternoon. I think I must have taken all the despair I felt and put it into waxing the floors and polishing the silver.

I got more work done in four hours than a normal maid would have managed in eight. The beds! The bathroom! The lot! I even scrubbed the front steps, would you believe? It was as if I thought I could earn my pardon that way…

It was a gloomy day outside. The lightest clouds in the louring sky were grey, and the muggy air was almost unbreathable.

The exhaustion hit me suddenly. I was scrubbing the last of the front steps when all at once I felt so knackered I sat down right there and then, on the wet step, panting as if I'd just run a cross-country race.

The blue-cushioned swing groaned on its hooks. The canopy's scalloped edges flapped lazily in the air.

You couldn't feel a breath of wind, though. Apart from that seat, everything was stagnant and silent. The litter in the street was motionless on the ground. I sat there, hypnotized by the sight of the strangely swaying swing.

Maybe it was Thelma's spirit that… Oh! I can see you smiling. Another crazy idea, right? And yet…

When I'd noticed Jess and his wife for the first time, the swing had been making the same rusty squeak, and I think it was that noise that had attracted my attention. A noise like a bird's call.

A little Renault van came crawling down the road, as if the driver were looking at the house numbers as he drove.

Instinct's a funny thing: as soon as I saw that little van I knew it was going to stop at our gate. And it did, pulling up next to the kerb right outside. Two men got out: two policemen. One of them had more stripes on his arm than the other. He was older too. Tubby and red-faced, he looked like a ball balanced on two leather boots. His subordinate was taller, dark-haired and olive-skinned.

I stood up to go and meet them.

"Are you Madame Rooland?" asked the officer.

Oh! You'll never know how confused I was there for a few seconds. Me: Madame Rooland? Someone had believed that I could be Madame Rooland? So my dream hadn't been as mad as all that!

"Madame Rooland is dead. I'm just the maid."

There had been a sort of nervous concern in the policemen's manner up to that point. Now they quickly became sullen.

"Ah, I see. Does Mr Rooland have a mother?"

"No."

"Or a father?"

"Not as far as I know. What did you want to talk to them about?"

"Your employer has had an accident on the Quarante-Sous road."

"An accident?"

"He went into the back of a lorry. It was stopped at a junction."

A calm came over me, just as it had the night Jess told me I'd have to go back to Arthur's.

"Is it serious?"

"He's dead. Hardly surprising: he was doing a hundred and forty."

The swing cackled in the garden behind me. Jess had joined Thelma there now. The pair of them must have been having a merry old time watching me standing there, swaying with shock between those policemen.

"Would you mind coming with us for the identification? We have to make sure someone hadn't just stolen his car, you see… It does happen."

"No need to change your clothes," the tubby officer assured me. "We'll bring you right back."

We left straight away.

"Aren't you going to close the door?" the dark-haired one asked.

"What's the point?"

They didn't insist.

I was on the back seat. The officer sat up front next to the driver and fired questions without looking at me, without even turning his head in my direction.

"Did he have reddish-brown hair, your boss?"

"Yes."

"And freckles?"

"Yes."

"Wearing a blue-and-pink-striped suit?"

"Yes."

"And a striped shirt too?"

"Yes."

"It must be him, then. Was it long ago his wife died?"

"This winter."

"Was he grieving?"

"I don't know."

Why was he asking me that? What did it matter to some fat old policeman whether Jess had mourned Thelma or not?

"So was he an idiot, then, or what?"

"What do you mean?"

"There were no skid marks on the road. He didn't brake. Visibility was excellent. A driver who was following behind him said it looked like he drove into that lorry deliberately…"

"Oh!"

"Your boss's death doesn't seem to have upset you all that much, eh?"

I didn't answer.

"He was American!" said the driver, with a knowing air, as if that would somehow justify my indifference.

I thought back to my conversation on the telephone with the secretary. I should have told her why the police commissioner wanted to see Jess. He must have thought they were going to arrest him. His wife had thought him guilty, just like me, and now the cops had come to the same conclusion.

Jess hadn't wanted to struggle any more. I'd made him feel like a murderer, and he'd just wanted it all to end.

"Was he a good boss?"

"I'm sorry?"

This time the policeman saw fit to turn his red face towards me.

"I asked you whether he was good boss."

"Oh, yes, of course…"

The car drove through the town-hall gates. We'd arrived. They'd left Jess in a little outbuilding round the back. The first thing I noticed was his feet, sticking out from under the tatty grey tarpaulin they'd covered him with. Jess's feet! The only man's feet that didn't give me the creeps.

I thought about how I'd shone those two-tone shoes a thousand times, using two different polishes.

"There's no need," I stammered.

But they didn't understand. They lifted the sheet anyway.

That night, when I'd gently stroked his mouth to feel the shape of his smile, the image of it had been imprinted on my fingers somehow. Now here it was again, still hovering on his dead face. I recognized it. A dried-up rivulet of blood ran from his ear. He had one eye shut and the other half-open, as if to take one last peek at my reaction.

"It's him, isn't it?"

By way of answer, I knelt down next to the body. The policemen didn't dare try to stop me, and I whispered into Jess's bloody ear:

"Oh, Monsieur Rooland. I didn't know you loved her this much!"

They made me get up then. They seemed awfully embarrassed about it all. Still, true to their word, they took me back to the house.

Their car turned the corner out of the road. I looked up at the empty home from the pavement outside. One of the upstairs windows had been blown open by a gust of wind through the front door. A curtain hung out of it, fluttering in the breeze like a handkerchief waving goodbye.

So, instead of pushing the gate, I continued on my way.

EPILOGUE

Two months went by. I never would have told you all this if I hadn't gone to see the doctor this afternoon, to do with some problems I've been having. He's one of the nice ones, you know: kind and understanding and all that. Plus he's known me since I was so high.

"My poor dear, I don't know what to tell you," he said. "You're pregnant."

He was expecting the usual bursting-into-tears act, but I didn't bat an eyelid. Just when you think something's finished and done with, back it comes to remind you it's not over yet! Still, it's a consolation of sorts to think that I'm the one who'll be able to give Jess the child he wanted so much, don't you think?

Oh, there'll be some drama back at Arthur's place, all right. Mum's hair will go grey overnight. She'll probably think there's some sort of curse on the women in our family. I don't care. It's too late now: she should've stepped in earlier.

It all would have happened differently then.

But that's just it: can things happen any differently from the way they do?

When you get right down to it that's life's great mystery, isn't it?

Anyway, it's better to tell yourself that it was all written in the stars. One evening, coming back from Ridel's, I *had to* walk past their place and see them sitting out on that blue swing, with their whiskies and the turntable playing "Loving You".

Is it my fault if my imagination ran away with me and I lost my head?

No, because it's all planned out in advance.

You'll never convince me otherwise, and I'll repeat it to myself every day, when I can feel the grief and the guilt coming near. Yes, every day, like a lesson you've got to learn by heart, or like a prayer: every day, *until I've forgiven myself for finishing off Madame Rooland in the ambulance, because I thought she was going to rat on Jess.*

———

Did you know?

One of France's most prolific and popular post-war writers, Frédéric Dard wrote no fewer than 284 thrillers over his career, selling more than 200 million copies in France alone. The actual number of titles he authored is under dispute, as he wrote under at least 17 different aliases (including the wonderful Cornel Milk and l'Ange Noir).

Dard's most famous creation was San-Antonio, a James Bond-esque French secret agent, whose enormously popular adventures appeared under the San-Antonio pen name between 1949 and 2001. The thriller in your hands, however, is one of Dard's "novels of the night" – a run of stand-alone, dark psychological thrillers written by Dard in his prime, and considered by many to be his best work.

Dard was greatly influenced by the renowned Georges Simenon. A mutual respect developed between the two, and eventually Simenon agreed to let Dard adapt one of his books for the stage in 1950. Dard was also a famous inventor of words – in fact, he dreamt up so many words and phrases in his lifetime that a special dictionary was recently published to list them all.

Dard's life was punctuated by drama; he attempted to hang himself when his first marriage ended, and in 1983 his daughter was kidnapped and held prisoner for 55 hours before being ransomed back to him for 2 million francs. He admitted afterwards that the experience traumatised him for ever, but he nonetheless used it as material for one of his later novels. This was typical of Dard, who drew heavily on his own life to fuel his extraordinary output of three to five novels every year. In fact, when contemplating his own death, Dard said his one regret was that he would not be able to write about it.

AVAILABLE AND COMING SOON
FROM PUSHKIN VERTIGO

Jonathan Ames

You Were Never Really Here

Augusto De Angelis

The Murdered Banker
The Mystery of the Three Orchids
The Hotel of the Three Roses

María Angélica Bosco

Death Going Down

Piero Chiara

The Disappearance of Signora
 Giulia

Frédéric Dard

Bird in a Cage
The Wicked Go to Hell
Crush
The Executioner Weeps

Friedrich Dürrenmatt

The Pledge
The Execution of Justice
Suspicion
The Judge and His Hangman

Martin Holmén

Clinch
Down for the Count

Alexander Lernet-Holenia

I Was Jack Mortimer

Boileau-Narcejac

Vertigo
She Who Was No More

Leo Perutz

Master of the Day of Judgment
Little Apple
St Peter's Snow

Soji Shimada

The Tokyo Zodiac Murders

Seishi Yokomizo

The Inugami Clan

ALSO AVAILABLE FROM PUSHKIN VERTIGO

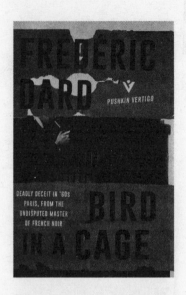
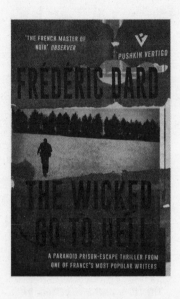

Willy Worries

how to massage, learn how to give long lingering kisses and have a sensual touch.

Because, at the end of the day, if you're worried about how you rate as a lover, it's not your penis you want to be considering. As a rule most women don't get the most sexual satisfaction out of a man's penis. Most women find it much easier to reach an orgasm by having their clitoris touched and stroked than by being prodded by a willy, no matter what its size.

Small willies can be just as effective or ineffective as big willies. It's really not the small piece of flesh in your trousers that matters so much as the big piece of flesh that's attached to it.

Success with sex and women is not down to what you've got in your pants, it's what you've got in your head that really counts.

A few lies about the willy

1. 'If you've got big ears you've got a big dick.'
2. 'Big feet are a sure indication of a big dick.'
3. 'Large thumbs mean long length.'
4. 'If a girl gives you a hard-on and doesn't make you come, your balls will explode or turn blue.'
5. 'Black guys have bigger dongs.'
6. 'The bigger your prick, the manlier you are.'
7. 'The fatter your flapper, the more fertile you are.'
8. 'The longer your length, the more sex you get.'
9. 'Women like sex better with well-hung men.'

10. 'Too much masturbation can make you infertile.'
11. 'Wanking makes you blind.'
12. 'Rubbing it too often can wear it down.'
13. 'Tight pants will make you impotent.'
14. 'Old men have tiny penises.'
15. 'You can't get a girl pregnant if you do it standing up.'
16. 'Sex is over when the guy comes.'
17. 'By just looking at his penis, a doctor can tell when a boy's been masturbating.'
18. 'Too many hot baths kill your sperm and kill your erections.'
19. 'Taking Ecstasy makes you a bigger and better lover.'
20. 'Alcohol helps you have better sex.'

All the above statements are total and absolute tosh.

No other part of the male anatomy causes such a stir or is so cloaked in myth and nonsense as the penis. So much rubbish gets talked about knobs. Maybe it's just a ploy to keep them interesting. The problem is that you don't get given an instruction manual when you grow a willy. So you have to rely on information from other willy users, who often haven't quite worked out what's what themselves. But instead of copping to the fact that they don't really know either, they make up some tale to cover themselves.

So what happens is that round the back of the bike sheds at school we all hear an awful lot of nonsense and often go on believing it for years to come.

NICK FISHER

LIVING WITH A WILLY

THE INSIDE STORY

MACMILLAN

First published 1994 by Pan Macmillan Children's Books

This revised edition published 2010 and reissued 2013
by Macmillan Children's Books
a division of Macmillan Publishers Limited
20 New Wharf Road, London N1 9RR
Basingstoke and Oxford
Associated companies throughout the world
www.panmacmillan.com

ISBN 978-1-4472-2787-8

A CIP catalogue record for this book is available from
the British Library.

Printed and bound by CPI Group (UK) Ltd, Croydon CR0 4YY